The Girs

A Journey in Memories Through the Self

story by The Father

Philosopher Stephan Pacheco

THE GIRL

The Girl
A Journey in Memories Through the Self

as witnessed By

The Father

by

Philosopher Stephan Pacheco

PACHECO **H**UMILITY **F**OUNDATION

Third Printing...2023

PACHECO **H**UMILTY **F**OUNDATION
WWW.LIBERTYCORE.ORG LibertyCore.us ManifestUtopiaBooks.com

Publisher-Stephan Pacheco
Editor-in-Chief Stephan Pacheco
Cover Illustration-jp farquar

Pacheco Humility Foundation
Reno, NV 89506

Printed in the United States of America

The Girl: A Journey in Memories Through the Self is a chilling tract challenging not only the ills of our times but also those throughout history. Not since Sartre and Derrida has there been such a thought-provoking work redressing the cycles and perplexities of social oppression. A tragic story of a disturbed, radical young girl, told through the eyes of the father, author Stephan Pacheco rattles the foundations of our long-held institutions. A gritty and bloody no-holds barred slap in the face to the self-delusional idolatry and manifestations of our times. A must read.

-Dale Jungk, Editor in Chief, Sun Rising Press

Dedicated to
all the great pieces
of unspeakable beauty
presented to a time
with an echoing recalling
that meant nothing
to anyone that did
not already understand
the endless perpetual bliss
that already existed in all things
that freely flow through us.
And so,
this, this piece presented to this time,
as all others that have
unfolded by the same nature,
means nothing.
As all things true mean nothing
and change nothing.

<u>Release</u>
A Warning Comes First.
Use your Life to Understand.
Life is Suffering.

WARNING:

This book is intended for the serious Spiritualist.
A strong understanding of Yin and Yang is recommended.
You have been warned.
It is your responsibility to gauge yourself, as always.
Remember, all experiences are yours to benefit from.
Fear, Anger, Offense, are your ego failing you,
MAKING YOU WHAT YOU DON'T WANT TO BE.

Introduction

Through careful and constant personal examination, the author of this book has determined that the human psyche is a malleable form. A form that can be deconstructed and constructed at will if people know the roots of their psychological defenses. It is not correct to access the mind from a remote point (a psychologist) to attempt to find a why that a psychological circumstance is rooted in. It is important to find out what happened within the body (not within the outside world) that triggered or set off a basic defensive response. What was the insecurity that refused the acceptance of reality? It is mostly unimportant to diagnose the reason that it is functioning. The response is always fear that yields insecurity that yields a cruel survival response of superiority that is carried out through a pattern of psychological defenses that reaffirm a fictional image that a person has of themselves. This seems to be a disease that has grown throughout societies, especially societies that are dependent on the manipulation of a populace for power, meaning the course of acquiring money. If people examine themselves, all of themselves, with honesty and without shame they study themselves closely and constantly in every situation and refuse to restrict their options by fear...then...It is absolutely possible to be able to reject parts of you that make you weak, that hurt those you love, that suffer under another's control. You need only honesty and an inward view. It is possible to not have to fight because you feel you must. We can understand that our thoughts, though original, are triggered by certain situations and are preprogrammed responses to certain types of situations. Situations that have built defenses (like fight or flight), and habitual reactions (that may or may not be repeatedly advantageous, meaning they may not even be logical, just reflexive). Our thoughts can be controlled if we can control our reactions to situations. Meaning, if you had cancer, or were stabbed, or were sodomized by police officers, or imprisoned by the self-righteous, you could take whichever outlook you wanted on the moment. Instead of feeling rage or dwelling in spite, you could feel sexual, or feel happy, or remain calm, or remain blissful. All conditions can be brought upon yourself in any situation, no matter what, if you could just let your imagination map yourself through the psyche to the point where there is no imagination, no hallucination, no need for protection, no image...and you could see the source of everything you think yourself to be. You can see that you are your own hand of fate. Every choice, every reaction, that has gone to feed your image was only meant to glorify yourself into power. And at the helm of whatever ship you may be at, if you have power you harm everyone around you. Everything you think you are protecting, you are crushing. So when you see it...how will you choose to remake it? Is it more advantageous to worship yourself, or other people, or nothing at all...or should you just live without the want to have the answer? The point is...we are all free. Right now. Free to become anything. But. Beyond the human form...There is something more. Something that is here now, that you are likely unaware of. Something beyond these thoughts. Something deeper. Something with you. A consciousness that exists at a point with less definition, so less restraints, a more pure point, uninfluenced by the Earth's conditions of survival. A silent- still -essence. Yet this point is controlled by the cycle of life and death, the transference of energy bodies. If you do not wake up from the bonds of your life, you will wake up from the most basic consciousness by dying and you can see it. That part that doesn't seem to die. Everyone will. And they will know the truth that their lives were not so important that they had to be so defensive, and trigger various forms of offense. This consciousness is reigned by yet another consciousness that is much harder to reach. Much harder to push beyond the undefined image of. Though it has and will be reached, again. So, there is more than one dream to wake up from. The choice to take the path of honesty and truth is the road of the rebel. Defying and recognizing, and becoming more than our original function.

The looser our grip on reality the more free we can become. Regardless of our freely chosen programmed reasons that justify the mess of our lives, or the ones we knowingly create to justify the greatness of our lives. We are all more deeply defined by our equality that can only be seen by those that have given up all identity and/or have died. And then these people can find more answers, but they will not likely be able to tell us.

Within everything you try to avoid, every thought you try not to have, within the pain you run from are the answers to everything you honestly want on Earth. Through the pain is Freedom. All we must do is always want nothing from the search, and we will always remain on the path to find an endless place that the mind cannot comprehend. This place is who you are.

Table of Contents

(Below is a map without coordinates. Be brave Quester.)

Chapter 1

The End

I hold her bloodied head in my hands. The interior of my hands feel so cold. It is such a contrast to the warmth of her blood on the outer part of my flesh. What a pretty red. Split wide. Her skin is so soft, like a fabric never made before, but similar to suede. My thumb almost sticks to it as I feel it. She has a pretty eye. I thought on her life. I thought of the sadness the slaves would feel on her life. I dropped her head on the cobble street. It made a thwapping thud, like a watermelon being dropped from standing height. I noticed as I turned away that it split open more greatly. I walked away. I began to forget about the blood on my hands. Blood grows so cold on the hands, so quickly. I always found it strange the way coldness deepens in the hands from an outside wetness. It seems like heat should come from within, not cold from without. I might remember her. Maybe when I wash my hands again. She was something different. I saw it in her just before I killed her. I saw everything in her. Like a flash as I held her. Her story seeped into my own. It burned me. It felt good to be touched by something. It is good to know that something that free had existed. I feel good. I feel everything about her. I feel her thoughts, her mind, I feel the essence of her, the very impulse that commands thoughts to be, the sensation of being that exists before and between every thought. I feel that pureness and that awareness that could dare notice such a location of the self. I feel her. I like her. I think I will remember her. I will remember. I will remember her life as she remembered it.   I walk onward through the shaded sun of the trees. What a beautiful day it is..

Chapter 2

Creation

She felt the folds of her vagina spread gently open. She didn't even know people called it a vagina. It hurt a little as fingers pushed against the narrow bones. **She was so young.** She continued to play with her wooden blocks. She let him touch her. She could have done anything to stop him. She could have yelled. She could have cried and he would have stopped. But why would she? She was never given the lie that what he was doing was wrong. He was only touching her. He was young too, maybe eleven. His hormones so racked and twisted into frenzy that he had to touch her. It was only for a short time. She hadn't even finished stacking the blocks. After it he held her. He rested his head on hers. He seemed sad. She did not understand why. He only touched her. She didn't want him to be sad. As he held her more tightly in the grip of his guilt, he held his head more firmly on her head. She said, "That hurts." He said, "Sorry," and he stopped. **Was she born like that? I wish I knew, but I don't make wishes.**

Chapter 3

The Child Begins to Die

In the early years of her short, short life she could seem so frail to a watcher. *Events come and go through so many lives, unnoticed, while other events rack and torture a mind for a lifetime. But what events are chosen? What turns us into the twisted, pained psyches that we are today? Do we have a choice?* Her early years were like anyone's, flashes of random events. Like the boy and how she felt bad for him. That never changed, even when once she was told it was wrong what he did. Perhaps she was told again, and maybe again, that it was wrong, but she didn't listen enough to remember when or by who. It was unimportant to her the first time. *Did she understand what she was doing?*

Her father...She remembered her father. A flash in a life. He laughed. When he laughed close to her, it shook her insides like a drum pounding sometimes could. He took her to the park on one sunny afternoon. A day like a dream. A day so far past it was like a dream. He laid her on the grass, it was fresh cut. It poked into her back. She pushed herself against it. It hurt. It felt so different than normal. Pain seared through her weak skin. Several seconds passed. She began to cry. A cry so loud, so shrill. People looked at her as she shrieked. Her father ran to her. Grabbed her up from the ground. He said, "Oh, I'm sorry little one." She stopped crying. She stared at him with a look of emptiness. *What pain could he feel? He felt nothing that she knew, even then. Why would he create pain for himself, guilt for himself, empathy for himself? He didn't even know he was doing it. He suffered when he didn't have to.* And she pushed him away. She never liked to be held. "Stop it," she whined as only a child or a woman trapped by her father can. He set her down. The girl ran to the distant side of the park. It wasn't so far away, it just seemed like it to her. *The illusion of distance. She still had that strange feeling of emptiness in her. She could not escape the feeling. She ran from nothing.*

Her running was cut short by a fence. She slowed when she saw it. She looked to her right for a way out. She looked to her left. She forgot about escaping *(as the mind often skips)* when she saw a group of young boys playing with ants. She ran over. One boy held a magnifying glass over the ants. He tilted it and turned it so the sun could shine through it just right. It made a tiny hourglass shape and in an instant an ant curled up onto its side and sizzled loudly. She began to laugh as the boys laughed. "That is a funny sound," she exploded. The boys laughter stopped. "Why isn't it moving?" she asked one that looked familiar. "It's dead," he stated. She stared at it. And then to the boys again. They seemed so much older than she did. *They knew what was dead and what was alive.*

"How do you know it's dead Billy?" *She had a brother. He had a name.*

"It's not moving," Billy replied.

"So. A lot doesn't move. That rock doesn't move. Did you kill it too Billy?"

"No it's a rock. It was never alive," Billy said.

"How do you know? It could be older than you. Or maybe you don't know what dead is." *The questions.*

"Shut up. Don't start that again. Jesus," Billy said.

She jumped up and ran to her father. "Dad, Billy and Mike, and that other boy are killing over there."

"They are just ants," the father said with a tinge of amusement and a dash of annoyance.

"I thought killing was bad?"

"It depends on who does it and to who," Daddy.

She walked away.

"Dad needs to talk with these other men, ok?" Dad.

Chapter 4

A Friend

From flash to flash...she must have lived between flashes. I wonder what was in between. What was the mundane? Isn't that as important as any other random recollection. It is there whether she remembers it or not. It was in her face, her eyes. One does not need memory to remember. One doesn't need the security of a story to exist. No creature has a full story to tell.

She snuggled in closer to the dog. The dog seemed old. So ancient. Her head laid upon the dog's chest. It was so soothing. So safe. The truck bounced down the road. She didn't notice the bouncing as she faded off to sleep with her friend. Her dearest friend. That she kept in communication with on a level so different than what we make ourselves have with people. As she breathed in tiny strands of hair she pulled in the easing scent of dog and pine and dirt. The dog's breathing consumed her as her head rode the waves of air. The mother turned back from the front seat, her hand gripping the father's shoulder for leverage and looked at her daughter. *She had a mother. A child doesn't have to be conscious to know what is happening around it.* She watched as her daughter's head bounced up and down violently to the trucks convulsions and then would gently rest upon her dog's rhythmic waves of inflating lungs. The mother spoke and she opened her eyes with a jolt. Then came the dog's eyes, quickly after. Her mother laughed and turned back to the front.

In the morning, she awoke with the dog. The truck was empty. She sat up. The truck was warm from the morning sun. *Of course it was cold, but it felt warm,*

because her body was much colder. She sat up. The dog sat up. She noticed pieces of shade throughout the vehicle. She moved her hand from the shade to the sun. She noticed the difference in temperature. She did it several times. Feeling the relativity. Her eyes grew wide and she looked up and around. She looked to her doggly friend. The dog had a look of desperation in her eyes. She turned her head in concern for the dog. She quickly opened the door. The dog leapt out and ran for a tree and began a short sniffing frenzy and then pissed. She looked around once more for her family and then climbed out of the truck. She went over to a tree and slid off her pants. She looked at the dog. The girl squatted down and pissed. She pulled up her pants and began to walk around. She saw the security of the truck and did not go far from it. She saw no sign of her family. In the distance she noticed other trucks. She decided to walk towards them. With every step she felt a pain in her belly. Her stomach made noises and she burped. She reached the other trucks, but there was no one there. ***What happened next? She wasn't afraid. That's the important part. It doesn't matter what happened next. She knows.***

The dog died when she was eleven. She walked up to it and called out to her. The dog didn't move. She had died. She thought of the ants. She remembered them. They didn't move. She thought of them because so many ants crawled out of her friend's mouth and into her eyes. Her eyes were shriveled and nearly gone. She couldn't see any emotion in them. She began to cry. She ran into the house and locked herself in the bathroom. She loved that animal so deeply. She cried. She felt the pressure from snot build up in her nose. She blew it out. She tried to be quiet, so no one would hear her, but everyone heard. She didn't want them to know that she cried. She randomly stared to a clock, she heard a "tick." She watched herself in the mirror. She watched what she looked like. She stared deeply into herself. She saw in her reddened, water-soiled face something that no one saw in her. She thought of the tears she had cried in situations she could not remember. She thought of her life. She thought of her dead friend. She thought of love. She thought of sitting with her friend, petting her. Being so comfortable with the animal. She remembered. She loved so deeply the only beast that seemed to understand her. The only beast that never hurt her. And she felt the death that took her friend. ***In an instant she first truly*** *felt infinity, in the void left behind in the death of something she loved. She began to actually understand death. Though she didn't know it yet.* "Tock." *A minute had passed and she traveled through an untraceable distance. Where are we really?* She pulled out of the journey that seemed to take so long. She pulled back from the understanding. *She wasn't afraid, but she was wary of the time change, of infinity in only a few seconds.* The crying ceased and she washed her face and blew her nose. She looked down at what lay in the toilet paper from her nose. *She realized its deadness.* It seemed pretty in its swirls and color. She threw it away.

Chapter5

The Mother Dies

"Mother."

"Yes Dear?" mother.

"I don't feel any sadness for you." The mother stared at her. "Do you think I should be sad?"

"I don't know," Mother.

"I don't think I should."

The mother stared at her. ***The staring didn't bother her. She did not feel threatened.***

"I know you are dying mother. I know that soon you won't be moving anymore."

"I'm so sorry," the mother cried.

"Don't be. You are not making yourself die. Maybe something else is. But even if you murdered yourself, I would still not feel sadness for you or for myself."

"That's very sad," Mother.

"No, it's really not. Why would I feel sadness towards a death? If what you think is true you will go to Heaven. You should be happy about that. And one day maybe I will go to Heaven. You should be excited about that. All babies will go there, so why not kill them? Right? Isn't abortion very positive, don't you save babies from sin by killing them before they have to live? You free them to God. Right?"

"Please stop. I am too sick to answer these questions. Enough of your games. No other Mother has ever endured such questions from their young daughter. Please stop," mother.

"You are not excited then?"

"No! I am scared," mother.

"Then you don't really believe what your mind thinks."

"Please stop. Please," mother. "Where's Billy and Paul?"

"Jail. I never realized just how much older than me they are until just now."

"Where is your father?" mother.

"Dead."

"No he's not don't say that," mother.

"You must accept truth mother, especially in your own death. There may be nothing for you. God may be something you only imagined for comfort. There are so many gods, you know. I think they are all imagined. I think that they're made up like any belief."

"Stop it. Stop it. Leave here. Why are you so cruel? What made you like this?" mother.

"I am not cruel. You are afraid. You are afraid to answer what I ask. You are afraid to think about what I say. In your mind you make me cruel, you make me evil, like you made your God, for comfort, for illusion. So that you wouldn't have to face these questions and comments, so that you wouldn't have to face yourself."

"I don't think you're evil. I never said that," mother.

"Even now you try to make what I say more comfortable for you. Your fear holds you back from pure thought, from truth, from the things you should be looking at. You try to redirect what I say, without even realizing it. Even now you try to create an image for how you want me to perceive you, instead of seeing what you really are. You are not an image mother. You are a liar."

"Stop it! Let me die alone then! How could you!?" mother.

"Mother. You will not have peace in death. I can feel it now." She rises up from the side of the bed. "Goodbye mother," She turns and walks slowly to the door. She turns back, almost with a tear in her eye. Almost feeling the sadness of humans again. "I hope I helped. If you don't use it now, maybe later you can remember what I told you. Maybe in some other form, in some other way. I love you. Thank you for living as long as you could."

She is changing. She is growing. The pain she gives is only from love. Where will she go now?

Chapter6

The Mirror Dream

In a bed she never laid in before she dreamt of a bed she had. She dreamt of the bed that held her softly in the early part of her life. She dreamt that she awoke in that bed. She awoke with fear throughout her imagined body. She felt it overcome her. There was something outside. There is something outside the window. Just beyond the blinds. She had to look. ***The hero has to look, she has to willingly damn herself.*** As the blinds opened she realized what it was that watched. Her fear ran deep. Her bones ached as she dreamt. The eyes of horror stared into her. Her eyes. Her gentle, child eyes, but warped with fury and strength. Her own image laughed in a way she had never heard. She heard cruelty. True cruelty coming from her mouth and directed exactly at her deepest sense of identity. ***Did she begin to believe she was evil? It is hard not to believe everything.*** The look on the outer one's face seemed purely to mock and cause pain. It winced and twitched. It came across her that it was a dream. She screamed, but no sound came out. ***No one could help her in this place.*** She screamed, she felt her throat ache as it suffocated her with convulsions. She continued to force it as she watched the girl stare into her. She began to make her body force her eyelids open. She pried them through pain. She fought herself out of sleep.

She awoke in the foreign bed, but not away from the thing that had hated her. Not away from that which frightened her. She woke up with herself. She woke up afraid of herself. She took a deep breath and let it out slowly, very slowly. As the knowledge entered her head while the breath passed by her lips, she knew that her greatest fear was herself. She knew that in every person she had seen so far it was their greatest fear too. She felt every "bad" thing that she could do unto the earth and all that lived upon the Earth. She felt it swell in her. She felt it flush over her.

Did the battle against the self, the ego, did this battle choose her? Or was her will to find something greater, beyond the false world of man so great that its momentum carried forth into this life from a past one? Is the battle for the self always within us? Or is her ego necessary to bring something else?
She is afraid of what she can and will do to the world. The girl senses the power of destruction. *It would have never bothered her if she didn't know it bothered others.*

Chapter 7

The Aunts

Her thoughts grow more fluent as she ages. Her brain is becoming stronger. The memories have more detail. The thoughts have other thought to support the story of the environment she is in. She is in a house. The supporting thought is that she is in her Aunts' house. Hhmmhh. The brain. Interesting. She is still so young. She doesn't acknowledge her youth.

She works. She works a great deal. The tips of her fingers are cracked open. They sting as she scrubs the floor, on her hands and knees. *She is very alone, but in a way that is different than most lonely people. She doesn't mind it. She is using it.* She scrubs and she scrapes the floor. Her mind wanders about, thinking of nothing specific. She reaches back into the bucket to her left for more soapy liquid. It seems to burn her hands. She notices an ache in her neck as she moves. She roles her head from side to side in an attempt to work out strain.

She stands and walks to the window. It overlooks a mountainous valley. The valley overflows with trees, pine trees, she thinks, but she does not know what kind of pine. She knows there are many kinds. Her father must have told her that. A squirrel loudly chats to another squirrel in a nearby tree. Such a beautiful thing. So free. So bushy and playful. It makes her laugh. *She begins to doubt that this is the way things have to be.* The creatures outside the window do not need all of the amenities that she receives by working for her aunts. Does she really need her aunt's home? Couldn't she be free like the squirrels? What must she do? She is not yet sure. What does she need to get to have freedom like the animals? She returns to work. She finishes the floors.

The girl looks down at her cracked hand. She looks to her fingernails. Some are longer than others. An emptiness comes over her face. She curls her middle finger and reaches for the cracked tip with the long nail of her thumb. She pushes hard into the crack. She does not grimace. **She knows that so many others have suffered far worse than she has or is. She is not dying of some unnamed, untreatable disease which has no means of alleviation, as her mother had. She is not in jail like her brothers. She was not tortured like her father. And their pain too was much less than so many others.** She stops pressing into her finger. She opens her shirt and looks downward at the scars on her breasts. She thinks she should make them deeper next time. **She will. To cut them slowly is the key to what she wants.**

Her aunts return home from their outing. She goes to the front of the house to greet them. As she looks out the front window, to make sure that the car was theirs, she looks out past it to the large lake that unfolds in a clear flat slate in front of her eyes. She opens the door and walks out to the car to see her aunts.

"I finished the floors."

"Good," said one of the aunts.

"That detergent burns my hands."

"It used to burn mine too. You will get used to it," said the other aunt.

"I want to take the canoe out."

"OK. Wear your life-vest and take your cousin with you," aunt.

"Alright."

Chapter 8

Nothing. It's First Pure Form

She went into the shed and pulled out the canoe. She looked around for the life-vests, but couldn't find them. She moved a few boxes and bicycles, but still couldn't find them. She went into the house. "Do you know where the life-vests are?"

"I'm pretty sure that they are in the boat.," aunt.

"I just pulled the boat out and I didn't see them."

"Well I don't know then," aunt.

She walked back out to the shed. She looked at the canoe. She rolled it over onto its hull. Sure enough the vests were there. She laughed. She pulled it down to the water and set it half way in. Sometimes she might feel angry that no one helps her do things, but it fleets away quickly, like a risen tide in an ocean. It wasn't bothering her at all today. She began to put on her life-vest. She hesitated slightly as she slid it on. It was cold and wet, but she had learned that to engulf herself in the pain of something meant the pain would end fast. She pushed her body to accept the vest, and she quickly grew used to the shock. But to even it out a bit more she seeped into the water.

She looked up to her cousin. He was still in the car. She yelled up to him. "Do you want to come with me."

"No. But I will," said the cousin.

"I don't need you to go."

"Yes you do. Your aunt said so," cousin.

"I don't care."

"Hang on, I'll go," cousin.

He ran down and sat in the boat. "Push off with that oar." He did, as she pulled the boat out into the water.

"Should I put on this vest?" cousin.

"If you can't swim."

"You can't swim. Is that why you are wearing a vest?" cousin.

"Yes."

"God. How old are you and you can't swim?" cousin.

"Thirteen."

"Are you afraid of the water?" cousin.

She looked down to the ground. *Looking into herself.* "I am." *She saw the fear.*

She climbed back into the boat and they paddled out into the lake. The cousin pulled out some goggles from his pocket. "I just got these," cousin.

"Can I see them?"

"Ya," cousin. He hands them to her. They seem nice. She takes off her glasses. She puts them on.   "Can you see without your glasses?" cousin.

"Watch." She puts her hand in front of her face and slowly pulls it closer. When it is about eight inches away she says, "I can see the lines in my hands right there."

"Wow, that would suck," cousin.

She takes off her vest and jumps into the water. The canoe shakes. The cousin clings to the sides of the canoe. "What the hell are you doing? You could have flipped this over," cousin.

"What are you afraid of? I'm the one that can't swim."

She sinks down into the water and pops back up. "I thought you couldn't swim," cousin.

"I can a little bit, but not to the point where I would say that I *can* swim. I can move a bit and tread a bit."

"Oh," cousin.

She takes in a deep breath and sinks back down into the water. She flips herself onto her belly with a great deal of effort. She stares down into the water. She looks for fish, but sees none. It is so quiet. She flips back up out of the water for air. While she has been under the water testing out his new goggles the cousin has paddled away. "Come back!"

"What?" cousin.

"Come on! Get back over here!"

"Just swim over here," cousin.

"I can't!"

"Then you will drown," cousin.

"Please!"

She becomes more frantic. She feels a wave of fear sweep over her. She flaps erratically in the water. A wave comes up over her head and she loses concentration. She sinks down into the water without a breath. Her eyes shut tight, as a reflex, not realizing that the goggles would shield her eyes. As she sinks down the loudness of her terror is silenced by the encompassing water. Her voice and the sound of her arms smacking the water are hushed completely. She kicks frantically. She bobs back up and cracks the elemental plane between her life and death. With a great breath and a sharp fluttering opening of her eyes she yells. "Help!!!"

He laughs. He sits back in the boat. She goes under again. She feels the fatigue in her body. Her energy drained by her short burst of adrenaline. The weakness in every thrust of her limbs. She feels pointless. She knows she can't make it to the canoe.

Suddenly all of her terror, all of her struggle...ended. It was done. It was so deeply quiet. Not quiet like she couldn't hear anything, but quiet like there was nothing to hear. It was silent. Every fear that she felt...every dream that she had...every will to keep herself alive...vanished. She noticed that she was above the lake. She saw without eyes. Her mind was not afraid of what was happening. She was at peace. Everything she ever knew...ceased. She was merely there. There was no place she had to be. There was nothing she had to do to survive. It was more pure than that. There was nothing she had to love. There was nothing she had to hate. There was nothing she had to save or condemn. There was nothing and it felt so full. What she had suspected all along seemed true. Nothing mattered. The gods. The histories. The words. They were nothing. Only dying, made up lies. She felt so infinite. So endless. It felt so light, and airy, but it was beyond that. There was no weight. There was nothing. Nothing. Nothing. Nothing. Endlessly empty. Endlessly complete. It was already what it was. And it could not be anything else.

Then, with no route, with no effort, she was back in her body. Within the silence of the lake. Within the terror, though it was different. ***What a gift is death.*** It seemed as if she was gone for such a long time, such a full time, that she should have definitely drown. But she did not. Her eyes were open and she stared through the water. She looked around. She saw the algae floating in front of her. The rays of light seeped in between the waves. It was beautiful. The buoyancy brought her up again, like the water was pushing her up from it. As she felt herself rising, she knew, she made the full decision, that if she went under again, she would not try to come back up. ***Nothing makes one more comfortable with death, than the gift of having nothing matter, and not by spite, but from the simple conclusion that it is true. And so she changed, even though she stayed the same, she certainly changed.*** She broke the surface of the water with a suffocating breath. The boat had drifted closer to her. She lunged for it. She missed. But found the final bit of strength to lunge again. She gripped the side of the canoe with everything she could. Her hands shook with exhaustion. She tried to lift herself into the boat, but couldn't. She moved herself to the front of it and slid her arm under a rope that was rapped around the front. "You prick! You fucking prick." ***Overcoming the barrier of shame hidden in profanity.***

He paddled back to shore. The shore was only about fifty feet away. It seems short, but it was not during those seconds. Her mind only wanted that boat, and it was much closer than the shore. Perhaps if she had just tried to swim she would have reached the boat without a problem instead of burning up all her energy struggling to stay afloat. ***But then what would she have gained.*** She climbed to shore as soon as she could touch the ground. She collapsed onto the beach. "You stupid jerk." She tried to hit him with a hand full of rocks, but she didn't have the strength to throw them far.

"I thought you were kidding. It looked like you were trying not to laugh. It looked like you were smiling," cousin. He pushed the boat back into the water and paddled away. She thought on his comment for a time. That must be what terror looks like. It is odd that terror looks so much like joy. Maybe there is not much that the body can look like when it loses control of itself.

She eventually worked her way to the house and her room. She changed her cloths and lay under her covers for hours. She thought on what she felt and why she still felt so eager to survive when she returned to her body. There were so many questions in her, though she knew now that they truly didn't matter. She still had them. How did she know what body to return to? What is the point? Of course, she knew there was no point. She knew death was only freedom. She answered the question of the eagerness to survive quickly. It was the human condition. It was the human game. Survival is what it does. There are a series of concrete variables that make something a thing. Certain things make life exist. We have a certain construct, one of the things is survival, another is that we feel gravity. Like water can only exist if it is two parts hydrogen and one part oxygen, or a car can only move with an engine, however that works she does not yet know, but it must be a certain specific way. *She gained knowledge, while others could have gained fear and paranoia for water. Her brain saved her. Her doubt saved her. She knew that all the views she had been exposed to, and through all the hypocrisies she had seen, that nothing was right. And if nothing was right, could it all be wrong? She has the way about her. She has the true knowledge. Where did it come from? Past life momentum? I don't know, she won't ever know either. One can deduce a great many things, but for the "whys" of things...We must accept that we may not ever know, for now, or forever. It is a technique best learned young, acceptance of final truth. Death.*

Chapter 9

Sitting Down and Working Hard

Her intellect was strong and deepening. Her understanding was vast. She saw what many great minds see only at the end of their lives. She knew through existence the truths that so many wrote. She knew the death that the **Bhagavad-Gita** wrote on. She knew the **Tao de Jing.** She knew it all, even though she didn't know these books existed. She wanted above all to deepen what she had felt. She wanted to surpass the lies that she believed, she wanted to surpass all that made her what she was. She wanted to feel at peace in the human condition. She knew that she was at peace in her purest form, as her spirit. but how could she reach it within humanness? How could she unite what she is in this world and what she is in the world she felt for a fleeting flash of endless time.

She set down with herself and entered her mind. She wanted to see if she could push through her voice and the visions she saw in her head. She sat and she sat, for about four hours every night. She sat in darkness. She sat, unafraid of what might be out there in the dark. She sat with herself, knowing that she was indestructible. She sat with her spine straight, like in the clichés of meditation she could see on books and in movies in her aunt's house. She wanted the deepest peace so badly. She would light candles and stare into the flame, not knowing that this was an ancient practice. She merely wanted to learn from the most base creations. Flame had no life, and it was very clearly life itself. It could not communicate, but it eats fuel, it moves, it breeds from one candle to another, it needs oxygen, it meets a number of assigned categories, but no one calls it alive. But it seems so pure, and to stare into it, it seems so deep.

In the first waves of meditation she would close her eyes and often see images. Most would be distracting, but she wanted freedom. Freedom no matter what existed around her. She knew she could have it, for in her drowning she did have it. She only had to drive through the mental hallucinations. For every image she saw, she looked for the darkest spot in the image, into the nothing of it, and she stared through it. She stared to the next image that would appear. She did it, again and again, with infinite patience. ***Patience is a technique that is often bred from the necessity of a desire that requires so much time, and so much distance. She moved, though she went nowhere.*** People had achieved bliss, why not her***? She had already felt it, she at least knows what the destination looks like.***

While she meditated, she grew the urge to write, to dance through the questions that tickle humankind's mind. Even though she knew it was irrelevant, she wanted to. It seemed like fun for her mind. And so she began to write. She wrote of great heroes that could live and die without fear. She wrote of wars and glory without guilt. She wrote of death and dying, accepting and surrendering, and never being defeated. ***Silly girl. What she writes is the same exact thing that one finds in Emerson's works, Thoreau's works, bibles, and so many ancient texts. She writes what has been written a thousand times, and that no one fully understood, but the original creator of the philosophy. And oftentimes not even the creator because they could envision their ideal but not become it, just as no one can understand what she is saying, until they are dead. Cute. Her great wisdom is that she knows she is irrelevant while these other's thought they were important. She is becoming what they understood. I shall try to find some of her writings within her mind.***

She sees into the irrelevancy of the anger she clings to, of the hopes she has, of everything that defined the reasoning behind her thoughts and emotions...
She began to understand that the hypocrisy of her mother and her father were irrelevant. However, if they had realized it their lives would have been more satisfying to them. Unfortunately, her mother died a slave. As for her father, she

had no way of knowing. She could not remember precisely what the hypocrisies were in them, but she knew that they made doubt in all things that could have trusted within her. If only her mother knew. If only she knew that it was all right not to know, and to admit it....***didn't she admit she didn't know***. She didn't have to be any way, she didn't have to lie about what she really was. The ideals of this world, the idolatry of fanciful desires, breeds a Society of Darkness that turns love into lies for the sake of feeling important to someone, to anything, to a child that will hate you for lying to ease its suffering and to bring it happiness. To know that fear often changes the true reality of things...Oh well. Her poor mother. Maybe she shouldn't have been "cruel" to her before the dying happened. Oh well. ***The girl has no need to have remorse over having no control. She is as much a slave as all of us. Trapped by circumstance and physical reality. It is important that she realizes that she can have remorse, it is just useless and creates pointless suffering for her.***

"Dreamer's Fire"

There's a passion in me:
something free and loud.
It feels like trumpets, drums,
and shouts of dreams.
Forever it's been in me.
But know it's loud   It's louder   Now it screams

Then my mind spins and flips,
twists and turns.
I think of what to change.
When and how to do it.
I scar   I bleed   I live
For what I believe.

But at the end,
when the music is dead.
Guts   Glory   Integrity   Honor
A man dies once.
Dream big.

Chapter 10

Art. Sculpture.

She realized in the loss of her identity and the revealing of illusion that she did not have to be anything she had been. She did not have to be a timid little girl. She could defy that. She could make herself as she dreamt. She could bend her m nd and that could bend her body. She could have the greatest of confidence in everything she spoke. She could relax her body and sit with such tenseness, as now she noticed she had. She was her own illusion to create.

She worked on it. She patterned her speech. She changed her hair style. Why not? It could have all fleeted away anyway into the lake. She belongs to herself now. She adjusted her posture. She made herself what was cool. She made herself assessable. She spoke to everyone. She didn't care what illusion their bodies sent out, like a jock, or a nerd, or an aunt. She developed a sympathy for humans that she never seemed to have before. *Maybe she did, she might not remember. Or I might not remember.* She focused even more greatly on overcoming the limits of pain. She cut into her chest deeply with a razor blade during meditation. Why not disfigure her body, it hardly mattered. She only gained strength from it.
She walked barefoot across the pine needles that surrounded the house. She made her statements sharper and stronger. She no longer had to know someone to speak harshly to them, to try and help their ignorance. Her entire personality warped. Her entire body warped. She became exactly what she wanted to be, with the exception of things she had to accept, like her glasses. But she did get a new pair. *She hardly even noticed when her aunts would help her, like buying her new glasses. They were just there. If she didn't*

have new glasses, it wouldn't matter so much.

She laughed. A different laugh.

Also, when she felt her mind cease to exist in association with her actual existence she realized that she could also make her mind or let her mind interpret anything anyway she randomly wished or specifically wished. She realized how the mind existed. How illusions formed within it. She could create for herself whatever personality she wanted. Whatever perception she wanted. She learned the trick. She understood the pattern of biases. Somehow, when having no mind, she could see it purely. By knowing that the mind was unimportant gave her the freedom to let it go and develop into anything, in any random second or any course of any time. She was not afraid to lose it or let it become something else. ***It is a tool of the masters.***

She presents an example. Her aunt babbled on and on about a miscellaneous subject the girl cared nothing for. The girl tried to explain gently to her aunt her own idiocy. But failed. The girl grew increasingly frustrated with the aunt. She felt it consume her. Then came a thought. "If this doesn't matter, why am I upset." ***She is aware, that is the most important thing in the beginning.*** She gripped the emotion. She held the frustration. She felt a warm feeling develop in the middle of her chest. She could not tell what was happening physiologically. She just knew that something was happening. She relaxed the part herself that created the neuroticness. She let go the pain and burden of frustration. She knew that it would likely arise again, but she also knew that she never had to let it. She could guard her mind from its own impulses. She felt for a moment how so many people don't understand that they can free themselves from themselves. "Worthless slaves." She noticed that too was an angry thought, but she chose to leave that one. She found it useful in propelling other activities that spun in her skull. Activities that she does not even let herself be fully aware of. She doesn't think on them much. She just knows that she will do it when she must. ***What is it? Her mind is so strong to control what certain parts of her mind know. To keep certain emotions away from certain thoughts, and certain thoughts away from certain emotions. Already she has developed the growing power to selectively, and precisely make herself, denying what***

any god may have wanted to damn her to. I wonder though, what would happen if her thoughts, emotions, her entire being that she currently is, could meld perfectly together? What if there is a balance? What strength would that make?

Chapter 11

A Physical Knowledge

One night while in contemplation her aunt gently knocked on the door. "Hi," aunt. The girl stared at her aunt. She noticed that the aunt didn't turn on the light and the aunt didn't say anything about the unusual position she sat in.

"We were wondering if you wanted to go camping with us tomorrow?" aunt.

"Who is going?"

"Your aunt and I," aunt.

"OK. Sounds good."

"Do you want to know where we are going?" aunt.

"It doesn't matter. It is all the same to me."

She laughed a bit. "You'll need to pack a backpack," aunt.

"What do I need to put in it?"

"You've never backpacked before?" aunt.

"No."

"Are you nervous?" aunt.

"There must be a first time to experience everything."

"True. Did you know that was an old saying?" aunt.

"No. I would only be nervous if I am afraid of failing, or if I was afraid of how you would rate my performance. And I don't care about either. What do I need to pack?"

"I will show you," aunt, "Come with me."

The girl and the aunt walked out to the shed. The blue shed. The paint peeling from the sides. The lock on the front that was never locked, like they were trying to keep something inside. She liked the way the sun lit up the shed, but still left shade throughout it. The light was present, but it wasn't there. Perhaps darkness is merely an absence of light. Light is a substance, darkness is not. It tickled her mind. ***She could nearly pinpoint the area in her brain that bred*** *the delight.*

"You can use this backpack. It was my first one," brown-haired aunt.
She looked at it. She tried it on. "It is too tight."
"It's adjustable," aunt. The aunt adjusts it.
"That feels good. I think."
"We'll see how it feels with 30-40 pounds in it," aunt.
Thirty to forty pounds did not seem like much. *Yet.*
"Here. You can use this mummy bag," aunt.
As it was handed to her she squeezed it. It was soft and covered with some
dust. She made a slight face. "We can wash it," aunt said without looking. Did
she sense the dust? Did she know the girl would squeeze it? Did she, the aunt,
just expect it to be dusty like most things she owned. *She always questioned
and questioned. Is this a key to her progress?*

Item after item followed. A large amount it seemed, until she thought of all the
useless crap that cluttered up the old house that she slept in. She was handed
no mattress, no stove, no *useless* books, or unlit, wet dripping candles. *But she
thought those candles were useful at a past time. Sometimes she will think
something is so great and later think the same exact thing is so pointless
or foolish, and later think it is great again. To many it would seem like a
contradiction. But she is freeing herself. The path of truth leaves no
footprints. She does not have to find her way to anything to make sense of
her own identity. It is untraceable, it is why the intellectuals cannot
understand the Existentialist way.*

"Pack it like this," aunt, "Your center of gravity is your hips. A man is his
shoulders. So the packs are packed differently. People always say that no one
is different, that all people are the same, but they aren't. Not men and women, or
any one woman compared to another woman, not by body build or brain capacity.
It is important to remember that when camping in a group. To know what
people's responsibilities should be, like map reading, and what they can carry,"
the brown-haired aunt said.
She noticed and remembered more detail and gave more tangible

manifestation to people that touched her at a certain time in a certain way. That is why she noticed the brown hair. And the words didn't just exist, but the "brown-haired aunt" <u>said</u> them. And she remembered, because the teachings came from a place of realness, not from fear or illusion like most actions from most people. It was factual or at least to the aunt's logical deduction of the aunt's own experience. It didn't repulse her.

 The hair shimmered. It seemed healthy.
"So, take this heavier stuff and pack it into the bottom of your backpack," the brown aunt, "And remember that every little thing has space in it. Like this pot and this kettle. So don't waste that space. Put some socks in there or this propane. Here let me stop. Go and get some cloths. We'll be gone for about four days, so get six pairs of socks. Two pairs of pants. Two shirts. A warm coat, maybe that blue one. And a hat. Get mine from the closet with the brim on it. You can have it. OK. Hurry up."

The girl smiled and stared at her brown-haired aunt for a fleeting second that would stick in her mind for a good lifetime. *A second stretched into untraceable time, lost to the abyss that naturally occurs from doing and thinking.* She gathered up the materials requested. She also grabbed a zip-up sweater with a hood for those nights and days that she expected might not be cold enough for the blue coat. She tried on her aunt's hat, now her hat, just before going outside with her stuff. It was a little tight. She tilted it forward on her head so it wouldn't squeeze her so much. With the hat on she made her way back to the shed. Her brown aunt had found a few more things. "It looks good," brown aunt. At first she thought the aunt meant the collection of camping things, but she realized the aunt meant the hat. She smiled slightly. "Fill in the holes of space with those cloths. Stuff them into the pots and such, and then we will reorganize everything in the house with the rest of the backpacks," brown aunt. The girl thought the brown aunt had said that before.

She stuffed everything into the pack and then lifted it up. She got it off the ground, but not enough to get it onto her shoulders. Thirty to forty pounds now seemed a little heavier. Brown aunt laughing, "Here try this." The aunt lifted the pack up and bent her knee in front of herself. She set the pack on her bent knee and slid her arm into one strap. And then swung it back onto her back finding the other strap without sight. The girl then tried. She was shaky and awkward but got it onto her knee. She was overcome with the weight at first on her knee and then more so when she swung it onto her back. She nearly fell over, but she got it. She took small steps as they headed for the house. The aunt carried the sleeping bag.

The girl plopped the pack onto the ground. ***Yes there is a physical reality to things too. Things have weight. The thought of weight was just a little jolt in her mind's recognition.*** "Let's go through the list and make sure we have everything we need," brown aunt.

The girl unpacked some of the things that were in her pack so she could see everything. She ran down the list. First the personal stuff. "Coat, socks, spare shoes, towel, silverware, toothbrush, hat," as the list was read the girl ran about gathering up the things her aunt had forgotten in the shed and from the linen closet, "suntan lotion, shampoo, rain gear, matches, sleeping bags, cup, plate, canteen, fishing poles, knives."

Then the stuff that was divvied up between the group; "lantern, the two tents, the personal one and the double, matches, propane, the big pot, the kettle, camp stove, dish soap, steel wool pads, hatchet, skillet, extra canteens, vitamins, worms, tackle. And now the food...enough for four days...Nutrition bars, trail mix, candy, four non-refrigerated tofu. That tofu will take the flavor of whatever you mix in with it, like hot cocoa. Hot chocolate, green tea, raspberry tea, three instant corn pasta soups, a box of instant oatmeal, grapes, cheese, bread, salt and pepper, hot sauce, instant refried beans and tortillas, mustard and mayonnaise packets, plastic bags, instant stroganoff, couscous, hummus, and salami," brown aunt, "It seems like a lot, but when you are expelling energy you need a lot of food. And we will be camping by a river, so we can filter plenty of water there. Uh, water purifier."

As the girl heard the list she thought to herself that perhaps she should get all of these things in her pack, just in case she decided to not come back. Or, could survival require less than this?

"Let's weigh the bags. That is always fun," aunt. They each drug their backpacks through the house to the bathroom scale. 40. 39. 27. The young girl could not believe her backpack was only twenty-seven pounds. ***She is deceived by her mind relating the physical world to numbers. She is brought to truth by reality. Reality weighs on her. Reality must not be forgotten.*** Due to the heaviness of twenty-seven pounds to her she decided to

try this trip first, instead of getting everything else into her bag. *Though she was still not sure if she would be returning. Is it interesting that she doesn't have any thought that would make her feel that she should tell someone that she is thinking of not returning? No, it isn't.* "Why is mine so light?"
"The food weighs the most and we are carrying most of it. We could have some lighter things, but we are not doing any long distance hiking," aunt.
"Oh. It seems like we need to eat less." The two aunts laughed at the sounds that formed words that the aunts could recognize. "How far are we hiking?"
"7 miles," brown aunt, "Now tie your tent to the top of the pack and the sleeping bag to the bottom when it is out of the wash."

Chapter 12

Freedom Exists in the Physical World

They left the following day after the packing. The girl was concerned as to weather she could carry the pack seven miles. Seven miles did not seem far, but twenty- seven pounds did not seem heavy either. ***Her mind deduced a physical relation, between the weight and the mileage. It seems mundane, but it is greatly important on the great path to be able to understand and anticipate where your mind might deceive you again. It is one crucial technique to taming fear and balancing the spiritual, intellectual, and physical illusions.*** She meditated on not letting the weight matter to her. Would it help at all? It should, but she knows that it will not prepare her like the action of carrying the weight will. ***Only by doing, will she be able to prepare herself for it. Contradictions are often simple truths. The mind does not need to understand what is true for it to be true. Perhaps human beings focus too much on one aspect of rational. Are there other aspects to be used? The mind is not the only way. It can make up the words, it can see it, but to understand it requires letting the mind go a bit, and sometimes completely. The hilarious thing is that, by letting the mind go, in this case, you are still using the mind, just a deeper, not so common way of using it.***

They drove about eighty miles from the house, and then four miles in on a dirt road. They parked the car by a gate and loaded on there backpacks. "Did we buy you those hiking boots," aunt.
"No they were my mom's. I don't think she ever used them." ***There are many ways to be influenced by what is and has been around you. So many unappreciated accumulated variables shape a specific random life.***

Sometimes it is just using someone's boots.

As the hike began, the weight of the pack was harsh to the girl. The aunts hiked ahead on the dirt road, occasionally looking back. Due to the newness of the activity it was hard, but she kept a steady pace, pushing through the difficulty. The aunts would stop and wait here and there on a log or rock that had a slight slant to it, as to lift the pack off of there backs. On the first stop, the girl caught up. "How far do you think it's been? Three miles?"
"No. More like three quarters of a mile," aunt.
"Holy crap."
"Distance is much different when backpacking. The weight slows you down and shortens your stride, and when you first start it is very hard to change your internal clock so it tells the right amount of time in relation to the distance traveled. Not that it is good to tell you because you will think of it, but you walk about one mile every half an hour. Just wait until we start going up hill," brown aunt. Laugh.

The hiking began again and again. With every stop that the aunts got to take, the girl pushed on to catch up, always just missing her chance to rest. She didn't know where they were going. The dirt road turned into a narrow path. They entered into bluish colored sage meadows. She thought she saw some deer in the distance. They entered aspen groves that rattled in the breeze. She could see the river now. It held a nice melody with the trees. All around her was a sense of quiet and unforced ways of existence. Many things she saw seemed only to be. How long had that tree stood in that same spot? How long ago was that tree chewed down? Did the beaver feel it scream? Did it matter to the beaver? Is empathy strictly human? Well for real empathy to exist you do have to know the thing that suffers. ***Thoughts distract her from the pain. But it does not elevate her beyond it. She recognizes the limitation in her progress.***

She noticed that they had passed three or four camp sites. Why couldn't they camp here or over there? Every step seemed so monotonous and useless. It all seemed beautiful and peaceful. Isn't this what they wanted to get to? How could one spot be better than another? After what seemed to her like a long time hiking, she knew that she had covered little ground. She ached, from her shoulders to her feet. All she could think to do was put the next foot in front of the other. Drive on. She thought, as she often did, others have endured far more than this. She pushed on. And with every step driven onto the ground ahead, she became more silent in her mind, because she ran out of things to think. There was nothing she had to do, but step. ***What good did it do to think of the pain over and over? That would only make it more tedious.***

It was strange to her, because it didn't feel like she was moving. She was not leaving herself behind. It felt as if she, herself, did not move, but every step moved her to something in the physical world that was more beautiful and more different than where her feet held her what was probably moments ago.

She came from a group of pine trees that hid a cluster of beaver ponds and entered into another grove of aspen. She noticed that several trees were carved with names and dates as far back as the early 1800's. She thought of how old these trees were. They did not seem that big. Her earlier guess on their age was wrong*. **She might have taken her own correction of knowledge as a bite at her own stupidity, had she been afraid of being stupid and had low self-esteem. But she wasn't, her perceptions were just wrong.***

Alone now, her aunts far from sight she left the trees and entered into a large area where no trees grew, and no water could be seen. At first she was inclined to think it was ugly. But she caught her initial reflex of past programming. She looked about and thought of the ancient rock and ground she walked near and upon. She stared closely at the sparse vegetation. She thought it beautiful. Her eyes drew from the smaller things to the mountains that surrounded her. She noticed as her eyes scanned thoroughly the surroundings that several waterfalls flowed down from atop the snow capped mountains. She laughed at herself. How could she think anything is ugly? It is all what it is. A rock cannot not be a rock, so perfect in its useful existence. ***Her biases. The lies she was told of what was beautiful and what was not tried to hold her from knowing that all*** *is beautiful for being exactly as it is, in its pureness, without the disease of having to think that it should be something else. A rock does not long to be a beaver, or vise versa. That is a human disease, from insecurity, made up by fear of not being loved. Brought forth by the disappointment that we are not perfect. Not being loved creates diseased want.*

As she walked through this barren beauty, so full of life, she saw that the trail curved down into a small canyon, where she saw the river and the trail disappear into it. Her aunts waited there for her.

"How far now?"
"I'd say we've hiked three miles. We've got a little less than four to go," aunt.
"But now we get to cross this stream. There used to be a rope across it," the brown-haired aunt ran her hands along the edge of the river and pulled up the rope. "It seems to be of no use."
"What if we got some sticks for balance?"
"That's the thing to do," aunt.

Everyone shed their packs for a bit and hunted down some chest high branches that fell on the ground from the trees that grew along the river and then proceeded to take off their shoes. The aunts took the time to role up their pants. One aunt headed across, her pant leg sliding down her leg into the cold water. Then the next aunt hobbled through the rocky bottom of the river, catching herself a couple of times with her sticks, one in each hand, as she slipped. The aunt's pants barely touched the top of the water, but since they were fully rolled into a bunch, the entire lower leg was soaked upon the unrolling of it.

The girl noticed the dilemma. She took her pack off on top of a rock so she could stand up easier when she put it back on. Then she slid her pants off, noticing a strong musty aroma rising from her crotch that seemed to make her feel good. Her first inclination was to touch herself, but she remembered the watchers on the other side. ***She was free to do it, but associated the physical world consequences with her actions. Maybe she will surpass that hindrance.*** She tied the pants and the shoes to the back of her pack, not noticing the looks of shock from the other side of the river. She reached through the straps, put a stick in each hand and stood up. She stepped into the water. "OOOHHHH!" The cold was sharp, but she exaggerated the sound. She did not anticipate having to push her legs forward and up stream at the same time, to fight the pressure of the current and the distance. The rocks were slick and she didn't see them as being as large as they actually were from above the water. She reached the other side and sat down to dry her feet and legs. Her aunts were shaking their heads and trying not to stare. They tried to accept what she did, but they weren't. Their social biases hindered them. But the brown haired aunt did seem to slightly smile and then turn away, clearly using a technique that "liberals" often use. The technique of caring apathy. The technique blocks the judgment of someone that a person cares for. However, it was clear that the aunt's mind was using this technique to deal with the situation. So it was not a willing technique that she brought forth from her conscious mind. The aunt didn't use the mind, the mind used her.

She slid on her pants. "I need some new panties." No one said anything, but they did notice the hole in the middle of the crotch. What they did not notice were the thoughts of arousal that swam through the girl's mind and body as she knew what she was doing was thought to be wrong. And what they could never have the insight to know, partially because they wouldn't allow themselves to have the thought and because they wouldn't dare look close enough to see the even slicing in the fabric indicating that she put the hole in her faded pink panties herself. It aroused her when she did it, because she new it was **naughty. This is her age of sex. Young. An age when her body was meant to breed. An age of natural filth and desire. Mostly uncontrollable to her, torturing, confusing, and absolutely enjoyable. She had no reason to feel the shame people that can't accept their vicious animal sexual tendencies have.**

The hike continued, with everyone dancing through their own heads with questions and answers that were complete manifestations of false reality, like how something should be or shouldn't be. But soon came the return to the practice of **mantras.** For the girl, she put the next foot in front of the past foot. And so the hike went on. Through cattle gates, and tiny groves amongst the ground, until finally when the pain itself became a **yoga,** the trees spread open revealing the High Meadow. A vast valley of grass, with that accompanying river running near its source. A huge granite cliff shot up from the end of the valley like a shrine to its own existence. Snow draped its crest. A breeze brushed the valley floor creating the illusion of a wave through the knee-high grass. The faint wind brought a chill to her from the distant snow. She accepted the easing chill because of the heat her body was generating from the exertion. She smiled and the pain fell away.

She made her way to the camp that she saw the aunts at. She slid her backpack off against a tree and lowered it to the ground. Her body felt so light when she pulled it off. She enjoyed the sensation of semi-floating. Her shoulders felt like they were expanding from her body. She flexed them downward, it hurt. **She flexed them harder.** She moved to sit beside the large fire pit. Her legs moved oddly. Heavily. And her knees seemed to swing forward like a pendulum she could hardly control. Her hip had a pain in it. *She is feeling levels to reality. She notices that the physical body that is in all of this pain seems separate from her. She feels fine, at peace, but her body aches, and she doesn't care.* She does everything she can to control the flopping leg, but she cannot. It is futile at this point. The body is beyond her control. But isn't the body what we think we are? Isn't the body what we define as ourselves? Then why does it feel separate when we cannot control it, or when we are in pain? Is it what we are? Is it something we use? Do we actually have anything? *The body will do what it wants, it is part of a physical code. It has its rules to existence. Its form is functional. For example, if she kicked a tree she might break her leg or bruise it. These are physical rules to the body. But it does not feel to her like she would be broken, just a leg. Just a leg like she would see on anyone. It would be the same apathy she would have for anyone's leg. Even though she could interpret the pain of the leg, it doesn't touch her.*

She may think the same thought over and over, but it is never repetitive. It is only repetitive to the naive observer. It is always deeper. Always new. Always more amazing and beautiful. Her world is her own.

The camp area was flat. It rose slightly above the meadow on a tiny plateau. Trees encircled it from behind. The river was soothing in its nearby babble. For a moment she rode the sound. She gazed out onto the view before her. The meadow did not seem so large, but she was sure it was. *The doubting of herself is the key to her obtaining new knowledge. The acceptance that she is ever-changing, and what she could have been a second, a year, or a lifetime ago, is as irrelevant and pointless as what she is right now, in the specific moment, and that is as irrelevant as what she will become.* "We are going to go fishing," aunt, "You can do what ever you want."

Yes, she can do what ever she wants. Yes. Here she can be free. The aunts leave the camp. As they walk away she notices that the other aunt has slightly blonder brownish hair than the aunt with the brown hair.

The girl set up her tent far enough away from her aunts so that she could do whatever nasty, or forbidden, or mundane thing she might randomly desire. She was pleased with herself. She had never set up a tent before. She shouldn't have been able to do it without instruction. Or so all the rest of the world might think. That was a great problem with the world, as she openly saw it, they don't have the courage to just think. They don't have the courage to just fail. She did not laugh a bit.

She went for a walk. Through trees and over rocks. Now, unconcerned with the "beauty" that was around her. She wanted the beauty of seclusion. A place where no one would ask what she was doing, or tell her how to do something they could not fathom. A sound filled her ears. Then a sight caught her eyes attention. She let forth a heavy breath that parted the air. She found herself a rock.

She sat by the lapping creek, lost to the white sound. Until a thought struck her, and she was lost to it for a time. She thought of the movies she had seen. *She can have thought of an event past, with no images or exact empathetic connection to an event she lived through.* She thought about the sex she had seen in them. Her mind was full of sex, so often. Where did it come from? Will she be able to free herself from it? But she likes it. Of course she does. She liked it a lot. She thinks of that boy that touched her, so so long ago. *It, the boy, the action, was not repressed.* She understands even more so why he did it. And he was probably younger than she was. Does the urge get stronger with age? Poor guy. *Though she didn't hate him in anyway or blame him for what he did, ever, it still felt like she forgave him more deeply. Maybe the emotional sensation existed in others around her thinking it was wrong and she picked up on that a tiny bit, creating a shallower sensation of*

reality than she normally perceives. It felt strange to notice it, the levels of the mind's perceptions. There is more than just one type of manifestation that the mind can create. One must be wary to not let the mind believe anything too strongly. The mind seems sensitive. ***She will feel the levels so concretely, but never be able to explain the levels. She already knows that her insights will make the sensation of non-attachment even greater for her, because no one will be able to understand her. To most people this would be sad and lonely, but she exists only in advantages. She will deepen and develop because of her lack of connection with people, all because she doesn't need anything. She doesn't need to connect with people. She already feels complete and doesn't need anyone to tell her she is complete. She is always in the positive of growth, only healing, never becoming ill like the others.***

She wonders how long she has been sitting on the rock, lost so deeply to thought. Her head feels like it has just finished pulsing. It feels a little tired. Her attention is quickly drawn back to her throbbing crotch. She must still be aroused. Often when she meditates she becomes aroused. Her thoughts engulf again fully into sex. She slides her hand into her pants, slowly, as to seduce herself. She looks around to make sure that she will not be shattering anyone's comfort, or her own for that matter. No one is around. She slides her middle finger into her pussy, though the hole in her panties. Convenient. She notices that her finger slides in easier than other times she has let the images in her mind fuck her. She is very wet. She undoes her pants with the other hand. She enjoys the greater mobility and bangs herself harder. She thinks of what that boy that touched her looked like. ***She has no idea. She manifests a face for him, without noticing that she does it. Her imagination simply creates it.*** She wants his cock in her. She knows what dick looks like. Her mind jumps to her cousin's penis. She thinks of those nights that he would sleep over. He never wore underwear and his night shirts often slid up, exposing his dick. She thinks that maybe he pulled it up deliberately. ***Or was that another cousin? And was that a pussy exposed? It is hard to know. The fantasy continues...***

Her fingers slid so effortlessly into her pussy, her own sweet pussy. She loved feeling the pubic hair covering her flesh. She loved touching her cousin as he slept. She fondled his limp penis back and forth in her hands. It did not grow harder. It was lifeless but warm. She noticed the hair on his balls. She grabbed them into her hand. She loved the feel of his skin. Soft. She wanted to taste it, at least to smell it. She slid down under the covers. The moon lit the room and lit his cock through the thin blanket that covered them. Her aunts must never have thought that such lust raged through these two young children. Was it not the same for them? The fact that they couldn't possibly think that this was happening made her even wetter. His balls smelt so good. She wanted him to fuck her.

She remembered pulling away from him. Happy and aroused that she had been so close to his cock, but ashamed, deeply ashamed. She silently punched herself in the face, knowing that she must stop. Knowing that no one could find out. Knowing that he probably would have liked it if he knew. But he could not know. She did not want to be controlled by it, she wanted to be stronger.

She stopped banging herself, quite satisfied physically, without orgasm, because she didn't know what one was. She looked around again. Still no one saw her. *Though part of her wanted to be seen.* She felt the guilt again, like she felt after touching her cousin. Why? Was it from her mother? Was it from all the people that oppress themselves and create the lie that sex is dirty and wrong, and should not be had with cousins and yourself? Where did it come from? She cannot remember. She wants to stop doing it. She wants to stop wanting sex so much. She punches herself in the face again. *To separate herself from it, to make her mind think of pain, to make the strength arise in her. It was all she could think to do.* She tastes the blood. She does not want to be a slave to her body's desires. But at the same time, she loves it, and knows she will do it again. She knows also, that she must overcome the guilt. Why would the human body love sex so much if it were so wrong? The guilt is more her enemy than the sex. *Can one indulge in the great pleasures of human reality, like fucking, like naughty fucking, and still be non-attached? Yes. The hero can. She must simply find the technique that allows it.* She punched herself in the stomach. She smelt her fingers. *Vast contradiction is what the great hero deals with, and becomes comfortable with. The great hero is fully human and fully divine, and fully mad. She is doing so well. Perhaps no one shall ever notice. I noticed little girl. How different it would have been, had they just noticed. But how could they, they don't have the strength to know us. And all they had to do was know themselves and accept themselves. And so our contempt grows in a flurry of our unobserved, unrecognized evolution into superiority.*

A lovely curse. Would we give it up to feel what they feel, to feel blind?

She returned to camp. It was getting dark. She saw the aunts returning in the near distance. "Have you been sitting here the whole time?" brown aunt.
"No I went for a stroll. What kind of trout are those?" Randomly, she noticed that she knew the fish were a type of trout. Where did she learn that? Oh well, who cares?
"Rainbows. Just little fellows, but enough for our dinner," aunt.
"Want to help me clean them?" brown aunt.
"Sure."
"I'll gather firewood and when you come back I will teach you how to build a fire out here," aunt. The brown aunt and the girl went to the river. The brown aunt pulled one of the fish off the stringer. They seemed to be mostly still alive. They were moving anyway.

"Take the knife, like this, and stick it in the anus of the fish. Cut upwards toward the head. Leave the jaw intact so we can put them back on the stringer." Some eggs fell out. "You can use this rowe for bait. Trout are carnivores. Take your thumb and push it up against the spine. Then you run it towards the head. And we toss the scooped guts into the water. It fertilizes and feeds the creatures of the river," murdering brown aunt.
The girl grabbed a fish and without the expected hesitation stabbed it, cut it, and scooped out its insides. It made her hands cold. She thought the inside of a fish would be warm. Normally she would hate all this instruction, but these were all things she could not know in the physical world without some sort of reference. This wasn't meditation, or understanding, or philosophy. This is base. Mechanics of humanness. ***She liked the game of living.*** She continued to

clean the rest of the fish. The brown aunt was pleased. She didn't have to work and she felt falsely important and that put her in a good mood. The aunt didn't know it was false, unstable importance, so it worked for the aunt.

The girl liked the power, and noticed her own look of mercilessness on her face as she cut into the fish, accepting the circle of death and that she was a murderer by design. It felt final and definite. Strong. But at the very same time she felt insignificant. Perhaps some larger beast could just as easily grab her, stab her, cut her, and scoop her insides out to make her clean. ***Random life. Constant death. For her...multiple levels and identification of emotions and the thoughts triggered by emotions.***

She returned to camp with the brown aunt and readied herself for more knowledge she desired. Knowledge is much easier for the mind when it is desired. First the aunt took some dry grass and some pine needles and set them in a pile within a circle of rocks. Then she formed a teepee shape of small twigs around the pile. Then a larger teepee of larger sticks. And a good sized log very close to the outer teepee. "One match," aunt. The aunt lit the match and set it into the grass and needles. The fire spread through the tiny needles and up into the first layer of sticks. Then to the outer. The log was eased into the burning mesh. Fire is so beautiful. A couple more medium sized pieces of wood were added after the main log seemed to catch. The teepee crumbled when it was used up. Poor teepee. Used and never thought of again. ***She amuses herself.*** For hours they stared at that fire. They spoke of irrelevant things. They ate the dead fish. They drank raspberry tea. It was delicious to the girl's tongue and warm to her belly. She noticed the many depths and flickers to the fire. The heat. The life. Every basic color. She noticed as it dwindled. She noticed as it was reborn with little additions. Eventually the aunts tired and they headed to their tent. The girl didn't notice when they had set it up. She sat by the dwindled fire and watched the bright streaks of burning coal race over the darker bases of glowing red and black burnt wood. It was beautiful, but cold. She went to her tent. After becoming well situated in her sleeping bag, it still smelt like detergent, she removed a flashlight from her backpack. She also removed a pad and pen. She wrote this poem:

"To Build a Man"

The fire in men
may burn bright and hot.
It may marvel others
with flickers of
blue, white, and orange.

But to build such beauty,
you must start small.
With twigs and grass.
Tiny bits and pieces.
To ignite the blaze
a spark is flicked.
Slowly it catches.
Soon it is large
enough for a core.
A center to feed from.
For an hour the fire feasts
on the hickory grain.
Flames engorge. Passers halt.
They marvel at the dancing heat.
The flame burns all it can.
But slowly it dwindles,
the magnificence fades.
The core is still there
burning red with passion.
Though, the heat intense,
the awe is gone.
and the gathered crowd fades.

Wait!   Look.
Someone has added
a twig, a tiny branch.
A handful of needles,
Some bark and some grass.
Flames engulf the accessories.
Blue, white, green, and orange
spread from one piece to another.
The little bits,
one by one,
become part of a wonder.

The tiny touches.
Will let the light
burn the night
and half the next dawn.
Perhaps, by then,
a new core will be needed,
but it is the simple additions,
A beauties kiss, a fatherly smile,
                a lonely hello
that gives a life its burning beauty.
These things make a man.

Chapter 13

The Camping Continues

The night passed slowly. She did not sleep much. The sounds of the forest were not peaceful and tranquil, but erratic and alive. She noticed as the night progressed that deer would pass her tent. She set up her tent in the middle of an animal path down to the water. The traffic was thick. The deer brushed the tent not realizing what was inside. A couple of times she tried to catch sight of them by peeping out of the tent, but they would leap up with fright and nearly trample her, vanishing into the darkness where they felt more safe. She noticed that if she didn't move around a lot the deer would merely move around the tent. And off and on she'd fall asleep and then awake. But this type of sleep was not so bothersome for her. It must have been the woods. She would rub herself and realize the distraction of her mind. The slight fear of being trampled was alleviated for a moment. ***She can perceive specifically what she wants in a situation. She does not need to recognize the random death that may soon await her. Issued to her by a large, stumbling buck.***

When she could see that faintly dimmed daylight had crossed through the dawn time, she decided to get up. The morning was sharp in its cold. A cold she had never felt before. There are different types of cold. The cold smelt different than the other types she had smelt. ***Too many times people miss the details. They miss so much of life.*** It stung the insides of her nostrils. The aunts were already up.

"What time is it?"

"Eight," aunt.

"But the sun won't rise here until about 9:30," brown aunt. The girl could see the sun on the distant cliff, like a spotlight on what was beautiful. She thought for a moment that the sun and the cliff made that beauty just for her. Then she laughed at her arrogance. *She played with the arrogance. It was natural as a human being to have it, but she knew it was stupid and useless. It wasn't real to her. It didn't even feel like a part of her, but she enjoyed it. Like someone would enjoy a cookie, or any other foreign object they might choose to indulge in.* She is trivial. *And that is what made everything so funny.* People think too much of themselves. She could see it in her aunts. She could see the hidden pride they felt because they were who they thought they were. They took themselves so seriously. She looked at the frying pan that they cooked with. She thought how funny it would be to beat one of them across the head. Not from malice, but to teach them. To destroy everything they felt they were. All that hammering of information, imposed identity, camping buddies. They didn't even see it. They need a little amnesia. She imagined the blow to the head. The stagger and the fall of the body. She almost laughed out loud at the flow of motion. It made her giddy. The blow to philosophy would be so great.

They all ate. No one suspecting the attempted murder of themselves by the girl. Though their bodies would not be dead, everything they thought they were, would be. It still amused her even after the time of eating passed. The aunts went off to fish. The girl decided to hike to a distant lake. She thought it did not seem far. The aunt said it was only about three-quarters of a mile. She had just hiked seven. What difference could it make? The lake was supposed to be at twelve thousand feet. She thought for a second. The aunt said that they were at ten thousand feet now. It really doesn't seem far. She must have taken thousands of steps to get to the High Meadow, and her steps must be at least four feet for a pace, or something like that. She took her notebook and a pen, some water, and some nutrition bars in a day-pack.

She headed out on a flat part of the trail. She could see the sun not far from her on the sides of the mountains. She could feel the warmth radiating off of the warmed earth. She hoped the sun would reach her soon. It felt so nice even so far away. There was such a nip to the shade, but the distant sun did make her feel warmer. She played with the sensation of heat on her face and with the cold that shriveled up her hands. She laughed, knowing that both affect her body, but do not really matter. She thought of the silence she felt in death and of the silence she had seen in other dead things.

When the trail began to climb she rested nearly every hundred feet at first. It was much harder than she imagined. Stupid body. It should be able to do this. She tried to hike further and further before stopping. She knew that she had probably not gone far. ***Not at any specific point, but for the entire hike. She thought it over and over. She had not gone far.*** She knew all she could do was keep going. The pain built up from the previous day and expanded in her muscles by the cold night soon lessened as her muscles warmed. She had an entire day, what else was she going to do? ***She might as well do something.*** The girl walked through the sun now. Oh the precious sun. It warmed her. She felt it all over her body. So soothing. It helped her. She pushed on and on. Her legs shook. She tried to drink only enough water to stop her throat from sticking to itself. Ahead of her she would see a point that she thought was leveling off. She thought perhaps water would be trapped there to form the lake she sought. But no. Again and again, no. It was beautiful though. Even the air that held less and less oxygen was beautiful. In the near distance she heard a babbling of running water. Perhaps it is a creek coming out of the lake? It wound through a clearing, just before the tree line.

Now the cold of the morning, that had turned into the warm morning, turned to the heat of the day. The heat she so desired made the trek all the longer. She laughed again to herself. First heat was good, now heat is bad. Heat didn't change. It was funny to her how she found it pleasant then bothersome. Heavenly then Hellish. She hiked on.

Over the final steepest rise, where it seemed that her body might not make it much further, her eyes caught sight of a crystal blue. Green grass surrounding it. She felt the coolness rise up from this piece of earth. She walked to the waters edge. She saw golden fish swimming so slowly through the water. She thought she might be able to grab one. But then how would she clean it? Well how do animals clean it? They don't. She bent down to touch the water. It was freezing. It felt good, better than the morning freeze in the air. She wiped her face with it.

She moved herself to a nearby rock where she drank her water and pulled out her notebook.   She thought of the hilarity of the attempted murders of the morning.   She wondered what had stopped her from enlightening her aunts. There was a bit of physical world practicality, like all the physical world consequences that might befall her.   **But she wasn't afraid of the consequences. It was more logical.** Most importantly, for the reasons to not do it, is that the action would have been wasted. The aunts still would not have understood the freedom and lessons taught. Oh well. She wrote a poem:

"Hammer"

The young man with the blue eyes
stood upon my street.
He formed the bland into beauty.
There was a grace to his tongue.
He spoke of the magic
trapped within dreams.
Of the heart. And of loving.
His voice knew freedom well.
It rang loud. It rang pure.
He was quite well defined.
Hours spent in study, I thought.
He must have a brilliant mind.
How he must have hammered
to develop such ideal.
Hammered all those thoughts,
with their malleable form.
Ready to recall,
for his speeches on the streets.
To hammer unto to us.
Hammer all his thoughts.
Hammer all his thoughts,
to a world which did not care.

Hammer. Hammering. Hammer.
Yes, I held it in my hand.
I held it tightly.
So I thought of it.
The handle in my hand.
I stepped to just behind him.
I cracked him in the skull.
Not enough to kill him.
But enough to rack his mind.
His mind so brilliant.
So developed. So right.
I killed that, in a single swing.
All which he thought he was.
He lay writhing on the ground.
With no name. With no past.
All that hammering gone.
Wasted time, I thought.
I smirked.
He knows only that he's here.

How fleeting is the mind?

After a time of undetermined passage she hiked down. She started out slowly. Trying to let gravity hold her back. After a bit, she began to let gravity take her a little faster. Shortly after that she was at full sprint. A sprint much faster than she had ever run before, because of the steepness of the grade. Rock and brush that covered the path added to her game. She leapt and landed steadily against the ground or a large rock that would ricochet her off into a continuing run. The momentum of the plunge aiding her recovery when landing on the ground. Most people would be tripped up by the momentum, but somehow she seemed to ride it. Mostly because she believed she could do it. The two hours of hard trek upwards, ended in a fifteen minute fall of unhindered joy. She laughed the whole way down, with little thought to wounds she would take if she fell. *It didn't matter.* Anything could happen to anyone at any time. *She would deal with the wounds, like anyone would deal with anything that might randomly happen to them at any point in time. The same time that she suspected might not exist, but the sensation is faint. Brought by the drowning, when there was no time. Though faint, even the weakest realization aided her magnificence, and her joy.*

She returned to camp and the experience seemed to blur. She spent one more night. She gained some additional skills and knowledge that her aunts bled to her from their minds. She accrued some physical habits, such as what she might bring camping, especially food-wise. She realized the ignorance of her aunts in many aspects of their existence, but she also had the logic to realize with appreciation what they did know. They knew a good deal about camping. She would hone their knowledge, and smooth their erratic camping style with her deduction as time moved. *Some things her mind makes note of. Other things it seems she just started doing. Though still, I know there must have been a point. We never remember the majority of what we are, how we became it. How can anyone cling so tightly to an identity that has no origin, and can end so quickly?*

Sometimes a memory consists of several memories, like the memories of camping. Perhaps she did not learn all of this on one expedition, but she certainly could not remember all of the expeditions in great detail. So many memories made one general memory. It seems to have a lot of detail, because it is a story. Many memories create the ability to understand through relation and experience.   This is called knowledge, physical knowledge, that with the power of logic in regards to making her experience more general and subjective becomes wisdom.

Chapter 14

The First Vision

As she returned from that long four days, she thought that it was not the time for her to leave society yet. ***She must be able to transcend the pain of a new situation before she may have the comfort it grants.*** She decided to take a hot shower. She always showered at off times of the day, so no one would bother her.

She often sat on the floor of the bathtub while showering. She liked the heat and the steam. She arched the shower water over her for maximum warmth and to not burn herself. The shower drowned out all noise and kept her warm while she was naked. She had been so cold and tired that she bent over onto her elbows and knees and then laid her forehead to the large porcelain basin. Suddenly she was gone. Like a flash she was running. Running through a forest. Beside her was a wolf. They were chasing something. Then, very easily she was seeing through the eyes of the wolf. She was the wolf. She had become it. She is the wolf. Her mouth aches with anticipation. Her heart pounds. She moves her jaw open and closed stretching out the pain. She can't wait to taste it. To feel the warmth run down her throat. She needs it. She desires it. She sees it. The deer. She lunges for its blood arteries, ripping out its throat. Joy and power brush over her. Her eyes bulge from her skull. She wants more. The girl wants to be covered in it....

She returns. She doesn't know how long it lasted. Did she make any noise? She moved in exhaustion so that the top of her head rested on the bottom of the tub. She looked down her body. Her pussy dripped with arousal. It is so much thicker than the water. She touched it. She ran her hand onto it. Across her clit. It made her twitch with ecstasy, it was almost like she flashed back to the killing. She rubbed over it, again and again, using her own fluids to decrease the heat she gave off. She orgasms in heaves, releasing power from her cunt. *She thought all of the profanity, not just these great words but all that is profane in all the world she felt in one great flush from her power. Her mind was everything that is power at once. And be sure it had nothing to do with sex.* Even though her mind screamed in pleasure, she knew she made no sound. The girl did not want to be bothered by her aunts, or draw their attention. She turned over and sat in the heat of the shower, unable to think of what had just happened to her, of what she became. Her body tingled from the release of power. *The First Vision.* After she had rebalanced herself a bit she shut off the water and readied herself for bed.

She decided to not unpack her backpack. She may have to go at any time. *There was a little less guilt this time. She did not punch herself.*

Some bouts of masturbation one remembers, but with so many in the hidden embarrassed lives of cowards and heroes they mostly all blend together into one swarm of rage and pleasure and peace.

Chapter 15

The Little Kittens

One winter morning when the house was very cold she walked out of her room after a deep sleep. She saw her aunts huddled around a cat that she had seen from time to time.

"Poor kittens," aunt.

She went to the kitchen to get some food. The aunts didn't notice her. She found some cereal and milk and then walked over to the cat. It was eating a wad of slimy purple mucus. "What's that?"

"It's the afterbirth," aunt.

"Oh kittens. They look horrible."

"They are deformed," aunt.

"They are? I just meant they're not very cute."

"They tend to get a little cuter after they are not so bloody," aunt.

"Their shriek is horrible too."

"We have to kill the deformed ones," aunt.

"Well someone does," aunt.

Everyone in the room stares at the little kittens for awhile. Watching them waddle about their mother looking for a tit to grab. The mother eases the wandering kittens gently into her mouth and sets them in front of her belly. The mother begins to clean and care for them.

"She's such a good mother too," aunt.

"I' I kill them."

"What?" aunt.

"I will kill the kittens."

The two aunts look at one another, back and forth and then towards the mid-teen woman. There was some relief in their faces, brought by the fact that neither of the aunts had the will to kill the kittens, but there was some fear and disgust in their faces too. ***She saw it. She didn't say anything, or make any expression in regards to it. Her mind simply gestured at it***. "We could just take them to the vets," aunt.

"Why spend that money? That doesn't make any sense. I will kill them. Do you have a pistol?"

"No," aunt.

There was a slight, but seemingly lengthy pause to the words of the conversation, but there was much mind spinning occurring by the three. "Just put them in a box. I'll take care of it."

The aunts gathered up the kittens and put them into a box. The mother cat screamed for them. She wandered around trying to find them. She would come up to the side of the box and try to take them out. The aunt took the mother cat and held it. She pet it sternly. "It will be ok, Boots," aunt.

"Please don't lie to the cat."

She grabbed the cats and went out to the garage. She set the box down next to a work bench in front of a large tool box. She began to feel her hands shake slightly. Was it adrenaline? Her heart began to beat faster. Was it fear? Was it anticipation? Was it all these things and more? She looked into the toolbox with a steady drive, knowing what had to be done anyway. Why would she not be able to do what needed to be done? **All this swam through her mind, as she drove through the action.** The first tool she saw was a wood chisel. It seemed sharp. If nothing else it could crush the neck. Why did this feel different than cleaning a fish? ***Familiarity with cat emotion and personality.*** She grabbed a kitten from the box, it was black and white. It looked cuter now. Her body felt cold. Her breathing was erratic, ***but she chose to not notice at the time.*** She laid the tiny cat onto its back on a wood bench. Its movements were like a robot, like animatronics. ***She thought of the word and animatronics and animal and laughed deep in her subconscious. She deliberately kept it from her conscious mind so that she could finish what she was doing.*** She laid the chisel on the throat of the thing. She felt empty. Her mind silenced. She pushed into the animal. There was a short crack sound, louder than expected. Her eyes danced, her heart sped up even more. Her hands shook and her vision slightly blurred. The cat gave a gentle gurgling meow. Without thought she turned and ran into the house. She ran past her aunts to the kitchen and grabbed a knife. She ran back by her aunts with the knife. One aunt thought "Don't run with that knife," but she said nothing. *Weak. Reigned. Prisoners.* The other aunt wept.

She reentered the garage. The tiny cat had rolled off the work bench. *She felt sadness for the creature, but it did not overwhelm her so she could not do what needed to be done. It seemed like a long fall.* She snatched it up from the floor. It struggled in the gravity to move and turn, not to escape the girl but to escape everything, all the painful life that engulfed it. She noticed the screaming cats next to her in the box. There were three more after this one. She gently laid the life-form on the table and sawed through its neck. Its cries hushed about half way through. It seemed slow, but it was fast. Bright red blood poured from the tiny corpse. Every cry from the box next to her lessened in intensity to her. She moved her hand up and down and felt the limpness of the animal. She grabbed a nearby grocery bag a set the kitten easily into it. Resting it on the bottom of the bag. She eased the bag onto the floor beside her, opposite the box. One by one she gripped the other kittens and cut steadily through the animals' necks. The cracks and snaps meant little to her now. Besides, a chicken being prepared for dinner makes similar sounds. *But it is different handling something that is already dead and something that you are about to make dead. The killing makes one feel more alive, and more connected to the creature that is dead. To kill is to understand the simplicity of life.* She tossed the others, two, three, four, into the bag. She set down the knife and walked into the woods carrying a bloodied bag.

As she walked, she thought on many things. Why did she feel so much anxiety? Why couldn't she simply kill? Does she really understand death and nothingness? Why was there an adrenaline-filled thrill to it? *When living in the world and interacting with life and death it is hard to completely free oneself from the ego's perceptions. When using the human body, there will be aspects of the human condition that still operate, but she must not let them bother her. And she will, learn to control them. I know she will. She wants the path too deeply. She wants the freedom from what rules her*

body. She does not want to drive through all those actions. She will develop. The important thing now is that she did it. She detached herself from everything she felt. An important technique.

She walked to the edge of a cliff, about a mile and a half away from the house and dumped them out of the bag. The animals will eat them. They will be happy to have them. She headed back to the house. About half way, she sat and meditated on her experience of emotion. She sat on a nice smooth, relatively cool slab of fallen granite, and leaned up against a tree that the rock had fallen against. She wanted the meditation so badly she didn't even notice the ants crawling over her. ***Good job.*** She steadied herself and more deeply rationalized the action. ***This is a world of death. It makes no difference how something lives, so long as it dies. But even if it doesn't that doesn't matter either. But parts of everything will always die. It is called growth and change, but it is death. Pieces of ourselves left in our wake of living.*** After about an hour, she walked back to the garage. She threw away the bag in a dumpster. She shoved it down the side so her aunts wouldn't be bothered. She went to clean up the mess in the garage. There was no blood, not even on the knife. It seemed like there was so much when she was doing the killing. How odd. ***Her mind exaggerated.*** All the blood must have been on the cats. The girl's eye caught a small drop on the concrete floor. She wiped it up with a rag and then threw away the rag. She left the box, it was in fine condition. She reentered the house. The knife didn't seem dirty so she put it back in the drawer. Later she noticed that the knife had been thrown away. She laughed a bit to herself when she noticed. How many other dead things have been cut up with that knife? And those kittens were fresh. How funny and irrational.

Chapter 16

A Human Connection

Some winters had passed by. Some summers too. Perhaps there was some sort of schooling that she attended, but it certainly wasn't relevant enough to her to make any sort of notice. When she was someplace mundane, or uninspiring, she stared out windows and onto floors, lost to the images in her mind. The glories she dreamt of. The people she would free. She thought of her father and how it seemed like he fought for freedom. *Is the fight for freedom genetic? Irrelevant. Perhaps though, but what one does with the war is not. What one can understand by researching and becoming free lies on the courage of not being owned by the thoughts and ideals of it.* She would like to know more of her father, she often thought, but had not gotten around to asking anyone. She would have the thought of it when there was no one around that could answer her question. *Random mind.* It was often in these times of thought, of imagination and manifestation that she would come across the reality of how alone she was. No one is like her. She would like to know someone like herself. She thinks that she never will.

Once, it seems that there was a man who sat beside her. Someone she did not feel that natural detachment from. Was he like her? Is that why she could feel him? He felt nearly real. She must have spoken to him at some point, or he spoke to her. *It is hard to find the memory in such thoughts. It is hard to find the development of a friendship. Has it always been? Did they meet before, somewhere else, or as something else?* He is familiar to her. They spent time together, but there are few direct memories of it. *Her mind ran at such a pace at the time, that she does not remember much. Plus, the*

physical world is not remembered so heavily by one that doesn't really care about it, but as an irrelevant game. He was like her. Similar anyway. He did not seem as irrelevant as most people do. When she spoke, he understood. It was the first time she knew anyone who understood the silence behind her irrelevant words. It was a relief. It held a type of joy. She was still alone, but not as alone. He called himself, Sid.

He did not assume to know everything like most people did. The funny part was that he does know more than most people. So does the girl. But they knew that what they could learn with and about these bodies and minds they seem to inhabit was a great deal more than they knew at the beginning of their association. They were often misperceived by anyone that would dare look upon them. They seemed arrogant, like they were superior to others. She was often called "evil." Sober people, and those pseudo-spiritualists the narcotics users, would often gaze at her when she was not staring at them and proclaim her as having an "evil aura," or some other such nonsense. ***This is one of the many consequences to enlightenment. To have no, or little fear (that is always being dealt with), will often leave people afraid of you.*** She knew she was not evil. She knew it did not exist. He was more passive in appearance. He did not seem as aggressive as she did to the fools. She would blabber what would seem like utter madness to people, and they would hate her when she was not around. ***And she did not care, but for flashes of her ego interacting with the earthly world.*** When she felt it, the ego, it would pain her deeply and she would have to move herself from it. ***Others are used to it, they don't even notice it, but to the girl it brought great pain to feel its blindness and stupidity.*** Sometimes it would make her feel randomly sad for people, because they could perceive evil and good. Other times she would feel contempt for them, for their lack of trying to understand anything. ***She had no way that she had to feel. She lived fully.***

Chapter 17

The Lack of Contempt

It was in this time blurred by the thinking mind that she began to camp by herself quite a bit. She would lie to her aunts, and tell them she was going with her friends, or with her cousin. She knew that the aunts would inf
lict their fears on her and try to make someone go with her. She did not need the illusions of security that come with groups. It made her feel sick to think how cluttered the aunts were with lies to make themselves feel comfortable.

In the far corners of the mountains that she would propel herself to, she found a great deal of peace. She did not feel the contempt or the sadness for all that she saw. And she saw so much. She saw every type of animal that her eyes could see. She felt no contempt for these beasts. She had no fear of the bear or the mountain lion or even of the bacteria in the stream that she would sometimes filter out before drinking. These creatures meant no deliberate harm to her, even if they did harm her. They were merely existing. And most importantly, she knew that the creatures knew this. They did not know things with just their minds, as humans so ignorantly do. They had a more vast reach and understanding of life and death and simple existence than the inferior humans that she attempted to hand any sprinkle of enlightenment to with wasted babble. She never had to speak to these creatures. They communicated on a much more pure level. These creatures she watched were more intelligent than most people she knew. She watched them. She saw them reason things out. Some were better than others. Some were stronger, some were smarter. She saw the same differences in humans. She saw that some species of a certain animal were differently equipped to deal with the world. Some were faster. Some were more meticulous. Just as humans are. Why does man need to separate himself so much from these creatures that know so much more than he does? Are they alike? When did the separation into superiority begin? The questions danced through her head. She would laugh when she knew she had no way to answer. The thoughts were gambits to amuse her, but they were not ever important, even if she would argue them. She learned from the animals and from her interactions with people that she could never teach anyone what she knew. They would perceive everything she said through their fears and biases. It made them weak and trapped. No one could fully understand her. The only way they could was to become her, or at least become like her. She knew that the animals could not become like her either, but at least they let her be. She noticed the difference between these free animals and the animals that she would see in the homes or around the homes of people. They were different because they were not so close to living and dying. But still they could communicate on a closer level to her.

Once while in meditation, she thought back on a cat that once lived at her aunts. She remembered how mean she was to it. It seemed weak and neurotic. It was skinny and sick. It was extremely sneaky, afraid, and so impure, so unhappy. The cat did not eat much. It did not clean itself. One day she found herself looking at it. It looked sad. She reached out to it. Surprisingly it did not flinch away from her, as if it felt the kindness being extended to it. She pet it. For awhile she acted kind to the cat. Over a short time the feline began to clean itself. It began to eat more. The cat turned itself into a thing that the girl thought was beautiful. It turned out to be a rare white Siamese. Its entire personality changed as well. Instead of sneaky and afraid it became gracious and loving. ***The realization: Animals have egos too. Egos that can be harmed and nurtured.*** The random things that affect an ego don't have to. One can become stronger than the ego and be free to perceive things without foolishness. To not be touched or phased by praise and acceptance or by cruelty and pain. ***Everything has an ego that gets to have the joy of interpreting the world. It is a tool, a device, that can control us, or we can learn not to be attacked by it, not to take it personally, and play with it. The important part to realize is that it is a designed thing. Be it designed by a god or by time, it does not*** *matter, but it is a form that has a function. A thing that works in a certain way, bound by the rules of the Earth, like a computer or a rainstorm. There are certain principles of function that must be followed for these physical things to exist, just as it is in the spiritual realm.*

In meditation she would sometimes analyze a subject, observe it, instead of trying to be with no thought at all. *Without knowing it, she used two ancient styles of meditation, the Hindi and the Buddhist. It was natural to her. She deduced through a simple, unemotional logic the ways to wisdom.* To be told how to be enlightened is to start out your journey lost. *That was her phrase, not mine. I think I will allow myself to speak it from time to time though.*

She continued to think on this cat and the animals around her. These animals of the forest have something different in their eyes. They do not have the fear in them. They have the different fear that lets them survive. They do not have the need for love. They do not have the disease handed to the "civilized" animals by humans. The illusions, the lies, the fear...Is it contagious? Is it society that breeds it? Is it that over consumption makes under consumption so much more severe in contrast? Can it be cast upon anything that touches the diseased society? Can the lies be handed to everything? The lie, the illusion that we have to always be creating something. The lie that man is happiest in victory? So many lies. Humankind is happiest when it does not need victory anymore. To need victory is to say, "I have a vast amount of insecurity that must be quelled with material illusion and fleeting validation...but what is that emptiness I still have...I need more victory." Nothing has to be anything. That is the ego telling us that we must act as a disease and infest the world with our self-righteous ideals. Nauseating. Perhaps she will begin to write philosophy now.

She is developing a disgust for human reality. She holds the world in contempt, because the people that inhabit it make what does not matter, matter. The world can exist in a pure form, she knows it. It can be free from the disease that has spread. Within all the contempt and humble arrogance she is building she still holds tightly the knowledge that no matter how caught up in her cause she gets, it will not matter. So, she loves all that she can destroy, and she cannot destroy what they really are anyway.

Why not destroy?
Why not fight everything that attempts to halt freedom? Why not try to cure the disease?

Chapter 18

Wasted Philosophy

The philosophy began. It flowed with the poetry. She began to develop a voice. Her first philosophies were ranting and violent. Angry at the weakness that people let themselves become. Single articles that she would send off to various underground zines would cover nearly every subject that popped into her mind. Slowly she began to realize that her style needed to be tuned for people to understand what she was trying to say. She was trying to say, "Fight." Fight for yourself. Be a nation unto yourself. Fight for your independence from anything and everything that would dare take it. She loved freedom. She loved the rant of freedom. She spilt it onto paper with blackened bitter ink to nurture the children of freedom.

The contempt she saw, the hypocrisy that she was engulfed with from day to day, no matter what miscellaneous person she encountered, made her ill. It made her write the philosophy. It was a reflex, like gagging. Sometimes she would run into people and discuss her philosophy. They would tell her how great she was, how masterful. Things she had heard throughout her life, mixed in with the random insults and mocking she would also hear. ***Both complements and insults were equally as useless to her.*** As she would hear them praise her or condemn her she would realize how they did not understand how to become what they loved. Young people spewed to her. The only difference between the youth and the aged is not philosophy, as most people might think, it is the young are so delusional that they don't realize that they are hypocrites. The aged realize they are hypocrites, but don't have the strength to stop their momentum built up from years of hypocrisy.

She saw the futility of her cause again and again. She saw that those that backed the great fight against all that assumes authority would only be backed with distant words, and would likely not take the action that it needed. It would likely not bring the destruction that she had accepted as inevitable to freedom. Anyone she randomly met and spoke with for a time, that she randomly had faith in, always faded away into the weakness they really were. People spoke at her in idealistic lies, not noticing reality. Always no one had the strength to do what should be done. Always was the world she tried to inspire lost to comfort and sloth. People did not have the strength to kill themselves. Perhaps, comfort and sloth are the ways to freedom. It is a type of freedom. But an empty one. She felt so isolated again. Sad that she would be able to give nothing. Depressed that she could not grant realization. The ego swept over her. Her mind chattered at her. She would meditate and rise slightly above the depression. But she would sink into it again. Why? She wanted. She wanted something. She wanted to give freedom, true freedom. But no one could understand it on a physical plane or a spiritual plane. No one could see that there was a difference, a balance. A game to be played, not a life that had to be lived. She often thought of her father in these times, but she did not know why.

All the rants slowed. Her voice was tired. Her hand was sore. Her mind ran too far away with her. She needed to leave the world that tried to make her care. It tried to absorb her. She hardly noticed it. She retreated to the mountains. *There is little memory of anything specific when her mind is trying to solve. She had forsaken nearly everything in her rants of destruction. The mind is powerful. The girl had to balance herself. What amount of time had passed? She looks aged. How long did this all last? In caring so deeply for the world she lost herself. She can grab nothing in her memory.*

Wait... She did try to love. She tried to love a boy. He loved her. She left him because she knew that she had to destroy. She tried to save him, but could not. He will always hate her. She must have had sex too. She lost her virginity...but it hardly touched her. She couldn't feel anything for the boy. She wanted to. She tried. Oh, she tried. Poor boy. He will never understand how she gave him up to try and save him from herself. She wanted to love, but could not love. She could not stop her mind enough to let him in. She wouldn't let herself be that selfish.

The mind is strange. Life is strange. Once I heard a man ask, "Could an enlightened man ever hurt anyone?" The answer given, "Yes, but he wouldn't know it." Maybe she is not enlightened like the answer giver thought you should be, because the girl always knew the pain she caused. Wisdom may be far different than enlightenment.

Chapter 19

The Teachers and the Students

Sid? Where had he been? It made no difference. She knew she had not seen him for awhile, but he was still there. Time passed strangely between them. Every conversation was like the first one, like they had never parted. Everything just carried on, expanding and evolving within themselves. It was an unbroken conversation that never differed in subject, no matter what they were speaking of. It was always of existence, depth and understanding. Always of destruction and endless love that gave them spite for all that could not understand it. Often they laughed at this contradiction. Man is so stupid, so blind. Missing all of humor in the seriousness we take in ourselves.
"I have found some teachers you should meet," Sid.
"Ok."
And just like that they journeyed away. They left their homes and relative families. They arrived at their destination. San Francisco, a town of trapped searchers. It was like an entire culture that started a journey to freedom, but stopped and got stuck in limbo. They were trapped by finding a place that was "good enough." A place that made them feel good to be themselves, and so they got trapped in diseased arrogance. Where one had to feel empathy about what everyone else felt empathy about, when, in fact, they should feel no empathy because the events actually didn't touch them at all. And they wouldn't do what was necessary to stop the events, like war and such, that they hated. They would protest and not fight. They felt righteous and so they too oppressed. At first it seemed like they were a tolerant people, but the girl realized that the culture seemed to push the "fact" that they were so tolerant. The girl thought the place was strange. There was something fake about it. But for everything she

did not like, she also always liked something about everything. At least, for a big city, it was a little laid back. It did seem tolerant in some ways.

She noticed the thought pattern of people was much different than where she was from. She laughed at the fact that no one noticed it. No one noticed that they lived in a completely different reality than someone from another culture, just by how they perceive things. So they lived in a different reality, but were still clad in the cloak of fear and they reeked of the disease. Still they oppressed for their own comfort. She noticed how different races walked beside each other, how different sexual orientations walked beside each other. It is like that where she is from, but people notice if a guy is black, or gay, but in this city people didn't even have that recognition. People were just people. But the catch was...people in this city have to be visibly tolerant. They have to call people "African Americans," or they have to call dog owners "dog guardians." The city took away the right to speak freely and to find humor in the gross or different. Like she had noticed before, it got trapped in a limbo. People felt they were tolerant, but they were as closed minded as anywhere else, but with a different guise on it. The people of San Francisco definitely took the world as a personal attack. There was so much fear, but at least it was a laid back fear, unless you disagreed with one to its face. It made her a little sad, but a little content.

She met with the teachers Sid thought might be interesting. She explained her perception to them. She told them what she knew. "I felt it, when I drowned. I felt nothing. I realized the pointlessness and fleeting nature of this planet. I realized the essence in all things. I meditated. I wanted to have it again. I reached through visions and thoughts. I found it. I found nothingness. It felt like everything. I stared through every vision that entered my head and came to blackness and then let blackness go."
"That's it," teacher.
She felt relieved, accepted. She felt, for maybe the first time, not so alone. She felt validated. She felt good. She thought that she may have found someone that had gone deeper than her, someone she could actually learn something useful from. She began to go to retreats and satsangs. She began to meditate in large groups.

As she sat in the large groups and emptied her mind from thoughts that divert her from her true nature she realized that it was much easier than meditating by herself.

"Why is it easier to meditate here?"

"You are using the dharma of the others. Their energy, their revealing of their spirit, is enhancing yours," teacher.

She would ask the occasional question, but soon realized that she had already or could come to the answers herself. ***Never trust anyone who would teach. In true meditation you gain nothing in listening to others. You only get trapped in their weaknesses. The girl implied it in her thoughts.***

"I once was going to ask you if I would lose cause by giving up what I gain here, but I realize that I lose nothing. I only gain cause because I fear less and less the consequences, nor do I crave victory or worry of loss."

The teacher nodded.

She was praised by everyone in the meditation groups. People said that they could feel the true love emanating from her. She would easily help anyone who needed it. People called her a saint. They said she would be remembered like that.

Even in the large groups she grew to feel alone though. Separate. The irony that she often laughed at was that she felt alone because she felt at one with everything. If there is only one, there will always be loneliness. Everything is in everything. When all is surpassed, there is only existence. And existence is always equal and non-diverse. ***She begins to see the consequences to enlightenment.*** Always in this world we must choose something, and we can never ever have everything. We must accept that.

Her mind is changing again. Exiting from physical attachment. The joy that swept over people that she saw when they first felt bliss, when they were first told that it didn't matter filled her with joy. So, she drove herself further into it. She felt great bliss fill her entire body and all around her again and again. It flooded her. It brought her into emptiness. She often felt that she achieved so much, but knew that there was more. The bliss she felt was ecstatic and eased her condition to the world. Her contempt fell away. All judgment passed. She noticed physical differences, like a black man and a white man, but thought nothing of them. The differences only lightly registered with her mind and in another instant were forgotten. *Her mind is becoming lazy,* but there is bliss. She was full of great energy, because she did not waste force on the deduction of the world. She understood its roots, its base, its essence, and she accepted it. With every deepening realization toward an enlightenment, she asked herself with the voice in her mind, "What aren't you willing to give up? What aren't I willing to give up?" She knew that to have true freedom she must give everything up. She must need nothing. She must want nothing. She must be completely free from anything that would reign her on earth. She must give up government, society, judgment, and more and more. To simply sit and meditate in a park she had to give up self-consciousness, and the fear of being attacked with her eyes closed. She had to let slide anyone's judgment that might be thrust upon her. If she was labeled "the hippie" or a "dropout" or anything, so be it. Every fear she felt rise into her body, she could accept and then release.

A fear that she had wrestled with and destroyed may arise again in another situation, though she could feel that the fear was weaker than the previous time she had faced it. She could feel her own evolution, her own revolt against and with herself. Within her was a battleground. And she fights and fights. Storm forth and cut into a soul and her psyche and devastate, and destroy. In this time of great battle, she learned and accepted that this world is a world of war and perpetual death. *She accepted it more deeply.* She saw the wars of the blood, and the more damaging wars of words that mangle emotions and perceptions for the weak, and the war for the soul that was fought between the physical world, the mental world, and the nothingness. In her world the nothing was now winning.

"What won't she give up?"

"What won't I give up?"

She sat in the shower of someone she was staying with for the weekend. A beautiful home, with a beautiful view. It smelt of Eucalyptus. She sat on the floor of the shower, warming herself with the water and trying to grasp what she had just felt only minutes before. Her mind exploded with thought. It pained her. It hurt to associate with the physical world. It ached. It stung. It was too much work. It weighed like rock on her neck. She fought. She pushed to have nothing. Then it was there. Emptiness. Total silence. Total being. It was what she felt in the water. Peace. Love. No judgment. No hate. Purity. She laughed the laugh that echoes through all things, across all creation it resonated and filled. From the shower she rejoined the group she was with. She saw all of there blocks, all of their fears that would prevent them from letting go of themselves. They all had to portray something to everything else. Whether they portrayed enlightenment or love, or intellect or control, she knew that they would never find the peace they craved. She saw that they would not give up themselves. And she knew at the moment of full realization that she must still go further. All the world was beautiful. She lived in bliss. She lived in peace. She was, at seventeen, fully enlightened, or at least completely non-attached. She could suffer a thousand minutes to help any human being on earth. She feared nothing. *It helped that she knew what she was looking for. She remembered the lake*. And so arose from the voice in her head, "What won't I give up?"

What won't anyone give up? All that she saw around her that at first seemed to her so much more advanced than most, so beautiful in their love...what won't they give up? In the laughter and the tears, in the gripping to the first stages of bliss...what won't they give up?
"What won't I give up?"
She went through everything she had to give up to reach it. Approval, hate, greed, the desire for physical pleasure *(though there was masturbation. Again, it can be quite sexual to meditate, but she didn't cling to it, she felt no guilt or sadness. She could exist and accept the physical world. The ego must not be so arrogant that it thinks itself so strong to not exist at all in the body),* identity, control, strength, **fatigue** *(all lost in the will to meditate for hours and hours, usually eight hours a day. To want freedom so greatly that you would push through all suffering. It is the path.)*...there must be more that has been conquered...*but she can't pinpoint it specifically. Her mind was not being used to record.* The path of truth leaves no footprints. *Why do you need to remember if there is nothing you have to prove, or nothing you have to be? When free, you do not need to remember. There*

is no identity that cares enough to remember.

She felt that she had often felt types of bliss before, but she knew always to doubt them. To always push them. "What won't I give up?"
"What?"
"What won't I give up?"
"Bliss." She did not want to give up this endless, timeless, sensation of god within her. She did not want to give up the beauty that she perceived in every existing thing. She did not want to give up what she strived for so long to have. She did not want to give up love. She knew that she had no choice. She could not be a slave to anything. She could not be a slave to control, to identity...to bliss...to love. The girl knew that eventually she would push and cling to the identity of bliss. She cannot be a slave. Or she will lose all cause. *Even in the bliss her cause was always freedom from herself, and now from everything.*
She left the meditations. She left the groups. She left without explaining to anyone what she had become. She knew that though they claim to accept all things, they would not accept her anymore. They would not believe that the great sensation of bliss, is a lie. They will not give it up. She began to rebalance herself in the world. She let the ego return, so that it may deal with the world. She re-began the usage of her mind. She could remember little of the time in bliss. It slowly fell from her as she surpassed it. Her humility is so great that she thought herself unworthy to feel what she felt. Even though she knew now, that she will always feel it. Without illusion. Without the lies of bliss. She would feel it in some way. She knew that in time she would learn to deepen beyond it and find the real truth of things. She would not be trapped in that false reality. *The ego can run away with the physical realm from time to time, but we must still accept the fact that we are in this physical world. We must not run from it. We must always keep it balanced, that is wisdom. Wise young girl, older than me. Older in reality. Beautiful.*

She saw that those teachers that seemed deeper than she was only went deeper into bliss. They only went deeper into escape. The teachers were helpful in much deconstruction of herself, but, ultimately, like all things in her world, they became irrelevant.

She looked back on her time in bliss and noticed that during this time she neglected earthly things, like eating, work, battle, etc. Where are her aunts? Where is Sid? Where is her poetry and her fight. It was time to return.

Chapter 20

The Endless Beginnings

She returned to the lake, to her aunt's. She touched the water of the lake. It felt different. The world will never touch her the same. It will feel like she is not a part of it. Always. She exists on earth, but expands far beyond it. She is everything and she is nothing. And she knows that she is the thing that exists that must fight. It is what she is. She stared at her reflection in the water. She has always known. Something told her when she was young. It might have been a red cloaked entity with a tiny black book, but she is not sure if that unnamed thing ever really came to her in her childhood. She might be quite insane. And after the meditation, she doesn't care if she is insane, or if anyone else thinks she may be. She lives in the world, unhindered. She feels the ego edging its way back in. She feels its power in this world. She feels the suffering that will mangle her as she struggles to fight in the earthly world and the spiritual one. She knows the pain is coming. She will use it, but she will know that it means... nothing. She will fight because she feels like it.

She walked into the house. Her aunts sat in the living room reading. They seemed happy that she had returned. They made her food. She participated in mundane banter. As they spoke she thought on her war for freedom that was brewing in her. She thought of how she cannot escape it. She also thought of how kind it was for her aunts to accept her and always to help her, even if they did not feel that she was going on the right path and that they mocked her behind her back. She thought of the war against all possessed by fear that hindered the physical and spiritual existence of all on earth. She wanted to stop all that assumed authority over anyone. The disadvantage to all the world is that she understands what death is. Nothing. ***This is what she thought as others talked.*** Babble for her to be amused. She thought of mentioning what her enlightenment brought her, but then she quickly thought of her curse of enlightenment, of how she could never tell anyone because they would not understand. She silenced the babble for a moment.

"Tell me the story of my father."

The aunts hesitated at the phrase that seemed to come from nowhere, but the brown aunt began to speak. "Your father was in jail for a year. But he escaped. Most people believe he is dead. If he isn't dead, no one knows what name he goes by. But either way, my dear, I think you should leave the issue silent as you have all these years."

"It may have seemed silent to your ears, but never has it been silent in me. I remember him. I remember now what he was doing. Your world calls him a serial killer, but if he worked for your government he would only be a hero. A controlled serial killer. It does sicken me how people like you attach goodness to something so long as it benefits you. You don't have to do the killing, so you don't think yourselves murderers, but you glean off the benefits you fucking cowards." ***Actually she thought these things, but she ran over the thought so much in her head that she felt as if she had said it. She controlled her petty emotion to gain the knowledge of her aunts and to use their home to sleep in for awhile. This is a technique, and is necessary when choosing to play the game of physical life.***

"Why was he in jail?"

Pause. Awkwardness. "I don't know," aunt.

She stayed in the house for a couple of days as she plotted the course of the game of physical freedom. She wrote this "series" poem to ease herself from specific thought.

"The Jester and The Pride"
Series IV
Part I

The jester looked back
a final time at the kingdom
he once held in gleaming eyes,
bellyaches and simple laughable dreams.
A sigh later, the jester, rode away.
Exiled from his home,
not by words of decree,
but by his own time.
His mind began to be.
He sent himself away.

Always loved, this youth was,
but always was he laughed at.
A fool, he was called.
And that he'd always been.
But time has a hideous nagging tone
and he heard her with every rise of night,
when the laughter died.
On Pride he rode away.

"The Jester and The Pride"
Part II

The jester, though young,
knew what he should be.
Or so his mind thought.
And in the same, he knew what he was.
So he thought.
The jester reached to be known.
He wanted his name to hold quiver and awe.
And so the jester rode.

If he stayed his palace was set.
He feasted. He was greeted at every door.
But some need trouble, not comfort.
Some need wrath, not laughs.
Some need both.
Those who felt to know the fool,
knew him not at all,
For this fool searched for cause.
Few fools ever do.
Only the greatest of fools ever find it.

Alone,
he rode. Pride, his horse,
heaving with every step.
Thankless, and never full of feed.
Pride paced on.

The jester did great things to let himself live on.
He did awful ones to survive.
But Pride held him fast.
His misery to strive, bred fury.
And it spawned into armies.

Sharpened.
Precision cut.
He became carved
in hard courage

He built the fate which bore his name.
When such determined fate is brought to man
it stands mighty—soaked in blood.

"The Jester and The Pride"
Part III

Lengthy and filthy the trail was.
To the castle it wound back again.
Unrecognized, cased in rawhide, now at bearded age.
The young fool was tanned with the dead.
He flipped his experiences off the back of his worn steed.
He scanned the land which held his heart at its first beat.
The jester's lips were unmoved for many years,
but in fits of madness.
The lips of this hardened man were peeled harsh
by the vile Irish breeze. Chapped to the point of pus.
They lay sewn tight together by solitary contempt.
But in time as the time became soft to breathe,
the jester began to spell the story of his name, long missed.
And of a new name, never known.
The murmurers began to gather.
The jester's voice grew loud and bold.
The volume spread as the crowd grew thicker.
The country's clown heard no laughter.
He saw eyes firm on his past.
Tears fell from such eyes.
Rage gushed from solemn voices.
The jester sat staunch in his tavern's chair.
The burns and the scars driven into his skin drew no smirk or chuckle.
He gave a kingdom of laughter a chance to feel life.
Some deeds he knew were dirty,
but bound in poetic psalm, they were glory.
In hardship the jester found cause and a soul.
To all who heard the tales, they were great stories,
but to he who kept them encased within his ribs
they became the soul's Pride Honor and Savior.
The jester bowed a final time. He gave nobility to himself. The fool exited a king.

Chapter 21

A Quest

Where is her father? Can she remember anything that might tell her? Is there anywhere that the family went when she was young? It seemed like she should find him, like he had something useful for her. She meditated and eased her mind so that it could remember far back. The docks. He loved the ocean. He hated the government, and anything that assumed power. She could hear his voice in her head, "This is not a free country. The government destroyed it with greed and fear and the need to control." The girl thought these words might be her own, but maybe she received some of her thoughts about the world from him. She cannot be sure. Where could a revolt be led from? It would have to still be close to the US. That's right. Mexico. A freer place. Baja. The Desert. A place where no one asked about the past and people accepted the stories a person told. Everyone there left the US for specific reasons. The town that they would visit when she was young...what was it? She gripped it. *Its name was not so important that she fully recorded it, but she knew how to get there.* A certain day came and she packed her backpack, and she left again. *But she never cared where she went, <u>she</u> was always there, no matter where she went. She never felt like she ever arrived or left anywhere.*

At some point she found herself driving a car. She was waiting for a train to pass in front of her. She noticed that many people pulled angrily out of the line of waiting cars to attempt to go around the train. She laughed. How long would it take them to go around the train? It would take more time than waiting. Why must everyone lie to themselves and think that action is the only way to accomplish something? Sad idiots. The girl sighed. Sometimes waiting is the most efficient method of accomplishing goals. *The philosophy never stopped. She felt it in all of the mundane. She always expanded on it. In any random circumstance. Sometimes she made note of it, oftentimes she did not. The thoughts only deepened her spirit.*

She had apparently traveled quite a bit. She had seen many beautiful things. But she could hardly remember any of it. *Perhaps this is why she traveled. She felt that she could only truly exist in the exact moment something was happening, when her eye first caught beauty. After that, her memory would warp it, and it would become useless to her, and she would leave it behind somewhere in her mind that didn't need constant accessibility.* Although her urge to find her father was prominent she made many side excursions with random people she does not remember, at least with any specific type of definition. *She felt them, but her mind didn't keep them in thought.* She often thought of how hard she was to explain to people, not her philosophy, but herself. *But of course her philosophy was meant to explain herself.* She never really delved into it with anyone, except maybe Sid a bit, but she could not remember with her mind the holy conversations with Sid. *A great deal of why she does not remember is because her mind rides her these days.*

She found herself sitting on the edge of an ocean. She rubbed her head with strong pressure. She tried to ease the pressure of her thoughts. *Her mind is so strong.*
She would have lived emptier if she left the mind behind with those that meditate. But she had had too many thoughts lately. Trying to plan. Thinking of how to play the game. Thinking of what to say to her father. Thinking of what to do with tomorrow. How will she eat? The mind runs away. She punched at the sand. She looked up to the sky. She fell back onto the sand. She felt the filth of the sand cover her, stick to her. It bothered her. It disturbed her to be dirty. She felt such annoyance. She felt such hatred for the earth and for its rules that inflict filth on her. She felt disgust for her own mind that built pressure in her skull. *She thought it. She realized it. She knew she could let it be something else.* She took in a deep breath that she imagined as light. She released it slowly from her lungs and imagined it as thought, and as blackness. The

pressure in her head eased. She stopped inflicting the earth with her bias of how it should be. She smirked and let out a forced breath through her nose that was like a laugh. She focused on the sand that stuck to her hair. She pushed her head into the sand. She felt the sand cover more of her hair. She lifted her head and thrust it hard back into the sand. She did it again. Then again. *She knew that her mind had separated her from her reality.* It made its own reality. *As if a thought saw a thought, she could see from a different place in her mind that the thoughts she was having were illusionary thoughts. Thoughts that were biased by her ego.* She knows that she is filthy already. She is part of the filthy earth. She rolled her head to the side of her face. She licked at the sand. She thought of the countless creatures that ate her skin, that cover her with disease. She thought of all that she had killed by bashing her head into the earth. Did this hurt the earth? Did it matter? Could she stop the pain? She looked down the beach. She sat up and punched the sand. She killed millions with every blow. She would have if she had walked on them too. She punched frantically, unconcerned with who might see her. *She thought of how unconcerned she was.* Then she stopped and sat quietly. With the mind she is destructive to herself. Without the mind she is destructive to everything else. Either way she knows that she chooses how the destruction affects her. She cannot stop it. Why not enjoy it. She let the mind start up again at full speed, but some other part of her kept a wary eye on it.

She wrote a poem around this time:

"Madness"

The howler's moon,
the full one,
lit orange through the haze.
Igniting again the madness
of those dark glory days.

The madness engulfed me.
I swung and I lunged,
with fist and through worlds…
I hit nothing but air.

As the madness grew tiring,
I fell upon the sand
as I dreamt of eating children,
I indulged the Devil's hand.
While I groaned in cruel pleasure,
"Animal is Man"

Chapter 22

Battle

Who was the man that rammed into her? He talked horribly to her. ***She let it seem horrible.*** "You are my little bitch, aren't you? You like it when I ram my cock into your cunt, don't you?" guy. How many times had she had sex? It seemed like a lot. She enjoyed the filth he spoke to her. It aroused her. She felt fluid spilling from her vagina. Her body rocked, she felt him inside of her, but she felt hardly anything of emotion. She knew that he did not matter. She wanted to feel more. She wanted to feel love. She cannot remember what it is like to love. Had she ever loved anything? ***It is always hard for her to remember what has passed.*** It was just a body that screwed another body. She thought of how often she got up and left after someone had had sex with her. She wondered why. She thought of it. "You fucking little cunt, you like how daddy fucks you?" It sent a tingle though her body, briefly interrupting her deduction. Is it her mind that runs over her emotions? Is it knowing that nothing is real? Why can't she feel anything? Stupid girl. Does it matter? It matters for the physical world, for the fun of thought. She came. She tried to push him off of her. He wouldn't stop. He wanted to cum too. He kept pounding her. Is this rape? She was consenting at the beginning, before she came, but she isn't now. It is rather greedy to want to use him, but not allow herself to be used. She let him pound her. She stared at him, his changing faces expressing the foul dirtiness that swept across his mind. He ejaculated into her. Should he have worn a condom? Oh well, if anything happens she could just get an abortion. Or give herself one, more likely. And if she got a disease what did that matter, it is only her body that would wither and die. It would be a great experience. She began to get up and leave. He grabbed her. "You aren't going anywhere," guy. She felt a bit of fear. ***At the***

exact moment of feeling the fear she knew it was because she had lost control. She felt anxiety. To remove herself from this poor young man that may only be playing a game, or he may be trapped by fear and insecurity, she knew that she would go further than he would. She felt it from him. She knew his weaknesses, like she instantly knew everyone's. Without thought she plunged her fist into his throat. She saw the surprise as she stared into his eyes. Her fear took control of her and she did it again and again. By the fifth punch, when his reflexes had been triggered by his mind, he was already dead and he could block nothing. She turned and ran. When she was far enough away she slowed down. She noticed that she felt something in her hand. It was a rock. She must have hit him with it. Her adrenaline made everything very hard to remember. The flashes of his pain were all she saw. It didn't bother her though. It had already happened. It was too late to matter. He had to deal with his own journey, including the random circumstances of his death, perhaps perfectly planned by fate. All she thought of was how she would like to stop the fear next time she kills a person, but still keep the adrenaline focused for strength. She felt high and low at the same time. She felt the power that made her high, and her own sense of mortality that made her low. But her true reality, that she accepts more in every second, was apathetic towards what happened. Her truth knew that it didn't matter. The prick did not matter. The guy did not matter. ***She repeated to herself to teach it to herself.*** And if any god tried to damn her for it, she would fight it as well as possible, but she expected no god would dare damn her when such random circumstance exists on this slave planet. She tossed the rock onto the ground, knowing that every rock in the area would not be brushed for fingerprints. She was completely at ease. She knew that she got to experience what everyone wishes they could experience when they watch movies and watch a character bludgeon some other random character. What an experience. She knew she could not get caught. She did not have to be tense, it wouldn't make any sense to be, it would be wasted time. And it would make her look like a criminal. So, she will be at ease.

She thought back to it. It happened only minutes ago. She couldn't remember it. It was just like in movies she had seen. The flashes. Images pasted in her mind, devoid of sound, empty of emotion, almost empty of action. Still and bright. The ad-enaline must have made her mind perceive it like that. Maybe she could make her mind remember the whole thing. She must have seen the whole thing. She watched it. *Sometimes she challenged herself, but never got around to actually doing it. Sometimes it was just fun to think of various things she could do, but it would not be worth it to do it. What would be the point? Her thoughts trail to something else.*

In a day that followed the sleepy event she thought of the news report. She thought of the words of bias and lies that no one ever notices. She thought they might say, "The victim, Senator Reid's son, was found today with his throat brutally collapsed..." Victim. Right. Why is the loser always called the "victim"? Why isn't he just called the loser. The Dark Society always teaches that killing is the worst thing of all things. *The only reason the Dark Society has power is by convincing a populous not to kill itself. It is how tyrants keeps power. They must have bodies and lives to serve them.* The dead are always the unfortunate. How foolish that lie is. It is far more foolish that so many believe it. We must know what we can be regardless of what someone so ignorantly might spew upon us. We have whatever rights we imagine and we must enforce them for ourselves. We have the right to just-cause, we have the right to adventure. If just-cause and the right to adventure are taken away, we cease to exist. *If just-cause and the right to adventure are taken away, we cease to exist. (I thought the phrase as I observed her thought.) We become a non-living part of a machine that propagates the security of power and civilization. Don't let anyone take away your right to reason and to exist. No matter what foolish consequences their weakness believes that they can enforce on you. Overcome their petty consequences. Do not take the spoils they offer you to put yourself in a cage.* Perhaps if the girl got crippled by that guy she would be called a hero just for surviving. How can random circumstance make someone a hero? How can loss make someone a hero? Nothing makes anything a hero. There is only life and living it. "Hero" is a word of the media not a word of reality. *To show preference in anyway, or to show glorification, is aiding the lies of power. The lies in our realities.* To be free, see no heroes. Even if you are that creature that pushes ever onward into war for the sake of everything else that you cannot physically identify as yourself, by label you may be a hero, but you are only a thing. Or rather no-thing. A nothing. Know what your label is and let it die. Don't lie to yourself. Don't worship your fake self. Overcome your own story of reality. And know that the cripple is just a cripple and that the conqueror is equally crippled by life itself. Never believe a label attached to anything. The only thing a name is useful for is categorizing for the more simple deduction of human thought. ***All brilliant thoughts spoken to no one lost within an electrical spasm of the brain. Where does it go when we are done amusing ourselves with it?***

Chapter 23

To the Ranch
(The Obtaining of Physical Knowledge to Aid Important Knowledge)

A bus pulled into a tiny fishing village in the desert of Baja. It had a smell that she had never smelt before. It was of sea and filth. She noticed it, but did not mind it. She walked through it, the town and the stench, for a couple of weeks. Not really thinking much of anything. She knew this was the town that her father was in. She knew he was close.

She liked Mexico. It was cheap, but more importantly for her there was little security. She stole food without worry of being caught. She took dresses and shoes. She even stole a tent from some wealthy Dark Societals. **She made the rule not to steal from those who needed something, from the poor, of those that could not understand how the world did not matter.** Mexico is a paradise for the unattached. She would visit the "American bars" at night and loot the wallets from drunken arrogant men that wanted her flesh for the evening they were in town. Sometimes she would have sex with them. Sometimes she would slightly maim them, but she did not kill any of them. She didn't want to make a mess. She just wanted them to know that she was there. A small wound on the face or the belly maybe.

She found herself talking with a man on the beach. He was an American. "There is no problem in the US. It is the best country in the world," man.
"Why are you here?"
"Mexico is a lazy place. Manana. That's my favorite thing to hear. I like to

vacation in a place that doesn't matter," man.

"Why does it have to matter where you live?"

"I have to survive. I have to make money. That is the great thing about capitalism. People can succeed," man.

"Eighty percent of all the money in the country of the US is controlled by three percent of the population. People can succeed in any system. It is only will that makes it possible. The system is irrelevant. It is the man that counts. All capitalism is is a tool to achieve power like any other societal order. It is all it is used for."

"You are an idiot. America is freedom because of capitalism, because people pay taxes for their government to protect them..." man.

"Cowards often lash out illogically. They often believe what they are told. They believe so greatly that they had thought of it themselves, contemplated the best thing, but it is limited and weak. Lazy, and simply, stupid. If you would become dependent on anything or anyone and pay them homage so that you could be dependent on them, you know nothing of freedom. You are worthless to speak to. Your mind means nothing to me. You are pointless." She began to walk away. ***She felt a physical irritation.*** Her arms ached and she held a pain in her chest. The man repulsed her with his stupidity. She knew that she shouldn't feel this way about him. She knew that he just wasn't on the path yet. All paths lead towards the truth, eventually. Maybe not in a specific lifetime, but they lead there, to truth. And besides, in the concept of infinity we are all already realized and enlightened, always. The truth is always there for us to realize it. The ego clutters it and makes annoying personalities and minds that are full of ignorance and lies, but the truth is still there, just covered. She eased her tension with a breath, but it was still there. She would have to work on it. If she was the same truth as he ultimately was it would be foolish to feel spite and rage towards his ego that didn't matter. He is what she is underneath the story. How could she be mad at herself? That is what he is, herself, the same essence as all things. How funny. A cosmic joke.

Man, yelling, "You remind me of this prick I met the other day. He took me to his ranch and talked about freedom in the same dumb fucking way you do."

The rage returned. She walked swiftly back towards him. He flinched as she neared. She swatted his arms and clinched onto his throat. They stumbled to

the ground, but she kept firm the grip on his throat "Who was he? Where is
he?" The man tried to push her off. He could lift her body, but he could not
remove her from the grip. He wheezed forth an answer.
"Four or five miles down the road in a campo called Los Olivos," man.
"North or south?"
"South," wheezing man, dying man, pointless man.
"His name."
"David," fool.
"Everyone has a use, you just need to know how to use them. Isn't this the law
of your Capitalism. Haven't I proved your theory?" She stared into his eyes, so
full of fear and confusion and blown illusion from the loss of control to a young
girl. "See this is why your society is shit, and the fakeness of all societies are
shit. Victory belongs to that person that knows they have nothing to lose and will
go further than anyone else. Victory is for those that can destroy. There is hope
this has taught you something. But you will not understand with your daft mind.
So you are deemed useless, and you are free from your traps that have
enslaved you, by that I mean my hand upon your life. Your life is lucky that I am
not like you. I don't need victory. So you get to live today." The terror in his eyes
grew. She found it fascinating to see such intense emotions from just staring into
the eyes. Her fingers cut slight holes into his neck. It looked like a little flute. It
was nice.
She left him. She reveled in her instincts that knew how to kill. She reveled in
her ability to be able to release the animal in her, or the ability to keep the animal
at peace. The sun felt warm on her skin. She liked the heat.

Chapter 24

A Man Given a Story

She hitched a ride to the campo. She headed for the ranch with the camouflage netting over the fields. There were several men around and a few women. All staring. Staring is a deeply rooted and finely honed tradition in Mexico. Three men walked to her before she could get to close. "Podemos ayudarse?" miscellaneous man. There was a pause, since she could not speak Spanish, maybe this guy couldn't either. The men fondled confusion back and forth until one of them remembered that he could speak some English. "Can we help you," man.

"Yes. I am looking for my father. Yo padre."

"No. No," the girl searched for a new rebuttal, "It is Mi padre. Not yo padre. My not me." She felt relief at the notion she was not being immediately rejected.

"Como se llama? What is his name?"

"His name is David."

"El Grande? El Grande is the only David here. I will bring you to him. Maybe he is your father. Many people have left behind many things when they come to here, to the Baja," man.

She followed the man to the porch of a cinder block home. "El Grande!" the man yelled. ***They don't knock in Mexico.***

A man opened the door. "Who's this?" the man that opened the door.

"Perhapes tu hija," man.

"What is your name?" the man who opened the door.

"Is your name David?" "Yes. Who the hell are you?" the man that opened the door.

"Do you remember the park. Remember the killing? The ants?"

The man that opened the door smiled, "No, but importance is rather random. You look like someone I might have known."

She smiled, "I don't remember the last time I saw you."

She reached out to hug him. He hugged back. He reeked of sweat and of other familiar scents that she had left far back into another life. He smelt like a grown man. She felt un-tense. It felt good.

They went inside the house.

"How did you find me?" dad.

"I remembered the town. I remembered how you always spoke of the free Baja."

"Hmmph," he smiled.

"What happened to you? Why did you leave the Dark Society?"

"I had to. I had to be free to fight. Um...I didn't want to harm you. I didn't want you to get hurt," dad.

"The last I remember of you is the forest and the trucks, with the dog. What was happening? I know something was happening, but I don't know what."

"I remember that too. We were trying to free some prisoners that had been arrested for wiring a court house, um, with explosives. How old are you?" dad.

Can we believe what we want to believe, whatever we want to believe.

"I don't know. Ageless, I think."

He smiled at what he thought was this girl's sense of humor, not understanding the depths at which she spoke. But she did not feel any contempt for the misinterpretation. "Ya, so, a lot of people were killed in the escape attempt. I was captured, but later escaped." Dad.

"Was Mom there?"

There was a pause. He stared at her shaking eyes. "Your mother was there, but she was just a lookout. She got away. I know she's died. I can sense it in you. It is in your posture and your tone in how you reach out to me. You can tell simply what someone is or has been and what they want to hear by what they give off. You only need know what to look for. Be observant. I'm sorry I couldn't take care of you. You would have had to run with me. I didn't want that. Who has raised you?" Dad.

"My aunts."

"How are they?" Dad.

"Good, last time I saw them."

"How long have you been away from home?" Dad.

She thought for a moment. Her mind could cling to no particular date. "I'm not sure, maybe a year..." her mind searched, "maybe two."

The father smiled and let out a breathy sound through his nose. The girl smiled. She does that nose thing sometimes too.

"Well, the media had labeled me a serial killer too. I had killed a lot of tyrants. There is no reason to lie you, it is what I am. I am not ashamed." Pause. The man searched for a thought. "I am sorry about what it did to you. I am sorry I did not get to see you grow up. But it looks like you did a pretty good job at raising yourself," Dad. She felt happy at the remark. Although she knew that there was no logical reason for this stranger to make her feel good. *Logic is not always useful.* She accepted the emotion.

"Did you ever see my TV show. I had one. It was a comedy," Dad.

"I don't watch a lot of TV. It clutters my mind."

"Oh," Dad.

"Did I have brothers? Yes. Where are my brothers?"

He looked down to the floor and then up to stare at the girl. He spoke like a storyteller. "They were executed by a police officer that thought he was a god for a moment. Later that cop shot himself, when he realized he wasn't a god. It's too bad. There is nothing worse than knowing that there is nothing you can do about something. I couldn't save them, because I wasn't there. They were robbing a jewelry store and the cop knew that they were my kids and if he killed them maybe it would stop me. I can't even seek vengeance on the cop. I have no satisfaction from it. Maybe they should have gone to your aunts. But I just have to accept it and fight on. There is no other alternative," Dad.

"Why did you take them with you and not me?"

His eyebrows squeezed towards each other. He rested his fingertips together and raised his hands to his mouth. "They were old enough, quite a bit more than you. You were also so much more innocent than they ever were. You were so fragile. You were so loving," Dad.

" I am not weak now. I made myself what I wanted to be."

"Good job. Are you hungry? How do you eat?" Dad.
"There always seems to be food somewhere. It doesn't not concern me that much."
"Are you hungry?" Dad.
"Ya."
As they ate she could smell it in the air. What was that smell? She knew it. Her mind translated the smell into an association with a label, a word, the word was "drug."

Hallucinogenic drugs. Marijuana, peyote, and mushrooms, and salvia divorium or the Divine Sage.

"So, what do you do here?" *She spoke already knowing the answer, but giving the father, figure the satisfaction of speaking. She thought that she could obtain more knowledge this way. Because she is not driven by random surface interpretations that are influenced by worthless biased emotions she could play the game of communication with exact precision, manipulating the minds of everyone for her own holy agenda.*

"We continue the fight for freedom. We grow the worlds undesirable cancers, like weeds, cactus, fungus, and sagebrush. We make the useless useful. We grow hallucinogenics. We provide the freedom of religion, and the freedom to pursue happiness, be it chemical or otherwise, to our northern neighbor. We provide a method for people to explore themselves and discover what they really are, no societal beast wants you to do that. It does not help society if you are knowledgeable about actual reality. We also make a lot of money," Dad, "If you are finished eating I will show you."
The girl noticed the stupidity of the man that was now her daddy. She had a natural comfort towards him, but that did not stop her rationality. He did not know for sure if she was anyone. He didn't know her at all. Was his guilt so strong about leaving her behind that he wanted the girl to be his daughter so badly that he made himself believe it? What did he leave behind? *Most questions never gain answers. We must not need to know anything. Knowledge can destroy insight, because knowledge is generally a lie from one person's*

mind to make themselves at ease with the world. There are too many lies to believe any of them.

They walked towards the gardens.
"I know you are my daughter, but even unto you I must tell you that I am no fool. If you tell anyone, ever, about this I will set you free from the oppression of the world myself with a mighty blow of physical oppression," Dad. *And sometimes questions get answered, sometimes we are merely wrong in our perceptions.*
She received a death threat that filled her with pride. She was instantly filled with joy at the proof that her father was not a moronic fool. Good.

She stared at the field of peyote. She quickly turned to the field of marijuana. She thought for an instant about killing her father and taking all of this growing money from him. Unemotionally and without crushing the thought down into her subconscious because she was ashamed or afraid of it she let it go, because it had no benefit for her. Who would she sell it to? How would she kill everyone else? It would be foolish to kill her father. *But she could have. Every option is always open to her. Love is often and of course ultimately the only option at the end of mental and physical types of death.*

"We have a lot of enemies, but none in Mexico. We benefit the financial community. We employ a tenth of the town. There are a lot of enemies in the US. I am sure you have heard that drugs are horrible things that can ruin your life. You can become addicted to them. Right? Never listen to anyone. Believe nothing but what you discover yourself, and still know that that is likely bullshit too. Anyone can become addicted to anything. Money, safety, comfort, the lie of knowing something, fear itself...the disguise of society...or heroine or cocaine, or Tylenol, or any escape. Anything, if you are weak minded. The only reason people are against all of it is because they were told to be, and people don't think past what they are told, no matter what they might tell you. And the man that happened to enforce this horrible lie of drugs being bad was Richard Nixon. He needed a reason to stop the Hippies. He needed to create a crime to stop a spiritual revolution that threatened to absolve all authority. The Hippies were physically peaceful, but they were threatening security, his security. They were doing nothing, but, they were doing drugs. So Tricky Dick sent in an organization called the DEA, the Drug Enforcement Agency. He saved his power, only to lose it later anyway. By the time everyone realized what was happening in the government, it couldn't be stopped, everyone gained too much power and money from it. People want to believe something is the truth, no matter who tells them. And may they help themselves if someone they love or want to trust for their own peace of mind and security tells them something, like a government tells them a lie. They will believe it with rage. Sorry, I may ramble on from time to time, or I may not, but you will have to deal with it," Dad. The girl smiled and nodded with each piece of his truth she received.

Over some amount of time she was taught how the various mind warping *(a positive thing)* drugs were grown. The lessons of experience were recorded like personalized formulas in her head for only her to understand, yet they were certainly translatable to teach anyone else. All growing on the ranch was done with the techniques of a laboratory rather than of a pleasurable garden.

Mushrooms. Psilocybin. A holy fungus that can explode a realized mind into understanding a piece of truth. A drug that promotes the sensation of unity and irrelevancy of the lies around us. Often comes the sensation that the hand is a separate entity from the self. It is a true sensation, but for the weak or unwise it can frighten them. To perceive the disassociation with the hand truthfully, one must perceive without the sick bias of fear. For example, one may choose to have the thought, "the hand is separate from the self, it feels different, unconnected, it is not what I am, I am not the body, I am free from the fears that the body can hold, what does it matter if the hand does not exist, it is not a part of me, it is nothing, I am nothing..." For example. *(Do not read the next indented part unless you are growing mushrooms, or have a knack for mundanely learning boring information.)*
And so she recorded the process of growing with the holiness of the drug experience.

The mushrooms must be grown in very sterile environments to keep molds from infesting their life. She can recall the wooden tables with three sides of plywood, just higher than the mason jars. Over the top was plastic, over the front was plastic with holes for handling the spores. On the corner of the front the plastic was held down with tacks to easily remove the jars. The majority of the preparation for growth was done in the plastic and wooden incubator.

She could recall the make-up of the solution used for incubation:

Agar Medium:

Wash 250 grams of unpeeled potatoes and 1/8 of an inch thick. Wash the potatoes in cold tap water until the water runs clear. Cook the slices until tender. Strain the cooking liquids through flannel with distilled water. Collect the liquid. Rinse the potatoes several times with distilled water and add the water to the cooking liquid. Get rid of the potatoes. Add enough distilled water to make a liter. Bring the liquid to a boil, then add 15 grams of agar, 10 grams of dextrose, 1.5 grams of yeast extract. Add the agar slowly or it can boil over. While the liquid is hot pour it into petri dishes. Fill them half way.

To start a culture of spores, put your spores into 10 milliliters of sterilized water. Shake well then add 90 milliliters of sterilized water. Shake it again. Pull some of the water out of the solution and add it to the petri dishes that have the agar solution in them. Add the solution to a few different points in the dish. Be careful to expose as little of the petri dishes to the air. Raise the lid just slightly to insert the solution. Let sit at room temperature for 3-5 days. Little rings form. It means spores have mated. Score. A bunch of little pure white mats of fiber will appear. Transfer these to mason jars that are filled half way with the solution in the petri dishes; that excludes the agar. Make sure that all jars are sterilized and all tools for transfer a sterilized. Shake the jars, for oxygen. Then loosen the lids on the jars and set them someplace, like a growing shelf and let them grow for 10-12 days at 70-75 degrees, depending on the type of shrooms one is growing. Every two to three days tighten the lids and shake them. With a saccharimeter, a device used to measure the sugar in the solution, watch for when all the sugar has been used up. When it has, harvest. Then dry them. In an oven at no more than 250 degrees. Then...take them. 10 grams is pretty good. *She recalls as if from a book. Which is probably where the man teaching her learned to do it.*

It is not important that she learned to grow drugs. She could have learned anything. She happened to learn to grow drugs. "What it is" is not as significant as "how it is" or maybe "why it is." That is to say, how it is she managed to use a brain to record it to a mind and why it is she chose to remember so exactly. She remembered only because it appeared useful to know. If her mind had not made the certification of importance she would not have remembered. Important knowledge memory is more accessible to be recalled, although all knowledge is remembered somewhere in the mind. The mind must also be flushed clean through meditation from time to time, or else the mind will simply have to give up from overload. This is why the mind begins to fleet away at older age and why geniuses lose their minds so early. They abuse the power of knowledge. Knowledge is made to be the thing that is important, but it is not, it is only fun for the game of life. Only useful for making comfort and usually power. It is a tool we choose to have. And all tools and techniques must have moderation, or else we become weak lustful gluttons. We must avoid the weaknesses already defined by other ancient scholars, like the seven deadly sins, in this random mentioning. Heed warning, people were smart before we were smart.

The girl saw that this knowledge of growing this particular thing, this thing that happened to be a fungus, was tainted with the need for perfection. The process needed perfection and specialization to be able to make money off of the process. It was precise and not plausible for any person growing for themselves, as should actually be done, in an opinion. A simpler method that she found while researching a segment of the world on the internet at a small internet cafe in the middle of the old Mexican fishing village was much more practical for the slightly-dependent-societal-do-it-yourselfer.

Order empty Myco Bags. Bags with self-sealing syringe orifices and breathing patches. Sterilize the bags in peroxide. Fill the bags to just about a half inch above the self-sealing syringe orifice with a basic soil mix containing sheep dung. Spray the mixture with peroxide to prevent mold. Vacuum seal the bags with a general sealer. Order spore syringes from a distributor, which is easy to find.

Inject the spores. Let them sit in darkness until the colonization period is over (the spore company will let you know what that is). Then insert into the light at twelve hours on and twelve hours off. Wait several months. And then get high and find a fake and fleeting sense of god. Use it to see yourself detached from yourself.

She remembered this method in a way she had thought it, not in a way someone else had recorded it to her. She often searched for the alternative way to do things on her own. She expected to always wind up alone again. Too much dies to expect otherwise. It is a world of change, and the great advantage to the hero mind is that it needs nothing, especially consistency, and so, it easily adapts--allowing the mind to think in any situation, one of society or isolation. It also did not bother her to have an advantage in the game by having knowledge that others may not seek out until they must, and that is even with the knowledge that knowledge is fleeting.

Chapter 25

Philosophers' Hearts

In a moment in a time of some sort, her father spoke of a grandfather. The grandfather apparently collected taxes for those that squander money to feel like they are making a difference, to feel important, and to unknowingly harm a society by doing the illusion of "good." The grandfather helped build the nation that father fought against. The father talks about the way there was never any ill feelings between grandfather and he. He just had a different philosophy than his father. ***Perhaps there is some genetics in the non-attachment to the Earthly world, or a karmic connection.*** So many countless hours were lost to philosophical blabbery between the father and the grandfather. It was one way that the father had learned to use many of the techniques of the mind, such as logic, and silencing egoic emotions (he did not want to lash out at his father). They sent words onto the wind. And they would laugh together. Laugh about how both were pointless at the end of their philosophy. And even though the grandfather focused on creation, the creating of a government, and the father focused on destruction, they understood each other. Both wanted to help the world. Both loved so deeply. As did the girl. But no one could hear them scream for freedom, any of them. The three philosophers all came to the same conclusion, that freedom is screamed for from deep in the depths of someone, and all the screaming around their ears will never free them. They must shut themselves up to hear the way. All three reached different levels in the creation of themselves. The grandfather, as he began to age, would have horrible nightmares. In the nightmares he would be trying to solve great problems, or simple problems, and he wouldn't be able to do it. He was thought to be a great genius with his ability to be logical. The grandfather was well praised in society, and still he was trapped by a self-propelling inferiority complex. He couldn't understand why his mind couldn't work the way it used too, the way he wanted it too. The father could not find an answer to give his father peace. But the girl knew. She wished she could have told him. The girl knew what the mind is. The mind is a device that interprets the physical world for the physical form, the body. The brain and the mind age and become less strong, less formidable, just as the body does. The mind and body that the young person abuses for pleasure brings the aging and the old pain and suffering. It is simpler for people to understand that we are not the body, but it is harder for people to understand that we are not the mind either. The girl thought back to the silence that engulfed her when she left her body in the lake, and the silence that engulfed her when she left her mind in meditation. It is too bad how people hang on to such false senses of identity. What we really are is much more simple, and the mind and body cannot help us know it. There is no device that we have on Earth that can aid us in understanding true existence. We only possess, for a short time, the ability to interpret Earthly things with our own limited personal Earthly devices. Our true existence cannot be comprehended by the mind. The mind is not functional in that way. It can be experienced and fully realized, but the mind cannot use the appropriate words to describe true existence. It is known in a place that most people will never realize exists. A place of knowing that does not involve the mind or the reflexes of the body. It is something else. Something that cannot be named. It simply exists, without the false names of humankind. Most people hate that about it, not being able to categorize it, understand it, feel secure with their knowledge. Knowledge is power, right? No. Knowledge is misleading, and falsely glorifying. Knowledge can be useful and used to assume power, yes, but no knowledge of the thinkers and the planners can be used to make anything that doesn't die. It is oftentimes a lie that makes us feel better about ourselves. She would have liked to have taught the brilliant grandfather. She would have liked to have told him that to "live," that to exist, a thing does not need the body or the mind. It is not what we are. She felt close to him in a way she couldn't fully understand. She never knew, and never will know him, at least the mind and personality part of him. Oh well, she laughed a bit as she thought on her grandfather. He knows now anything she could have told him. How funny her want was to her. How foolish. She laughed it away with full out laughter. Her father looked at her with concern as she did this, because he did not say anything amusing. She didn't notice. She didn't notice a lot of things that were unimportant.

As her father spoke of the accessories he had seen in life, she thought of how familiar he was to her. Calm and soothing in his dramatic tone and excessive arm flailing. She noticed that she should not be feeling calm around a blatant psychotic, but she often felt that way. But for him there was even more calmness. She knew him, and in a different way than she knows a portion of all things. She knew him as her dad. She remembers the love that seemed more steady back in the blurred days of her extreme youth. She loves her dad. She loves what he existed as. She never had a moment of judging for anything that he did. If anything there was more approval for it, for the levels of freedom he attained. She didn't speak much of herself in the discourse, though she had thought she would have. She just listened to her dad.

"Why did you kill all of those people?"
"Why wouldn't I have? They would not bring themselves into the proper evolutionary point where they could understand what I was saying. I had no other logical choice. In order to cure their disease I had to destroy the disease in them. They wouldn't cure themselves. I had to destroy them, for the sake of the world's freedom. It had become incurable. And they inflicted the disease onto others, the disease of fear, with the technique of denying other's freedom so that they themselves can feel comfortable. They offered the disease like poisonous candy under the lie of law and order. They were blinded by their need to feel secure, feel control. They destroyed the world around them with their fear. It is not my fault that they could not understand death. It is not my fault that they didn't win. It is not my fault that they could not evolve. It is their fault. I would not hold any qualm against them if they had killed me, my journey, as I currently know it, would have simply been over. Right? (*It sounds like she is talking. Is what she is handed down from the father, like all other types of fear based diseases? If fear can be handed down, why not wisdom. Is she afraid? It doesn't seem like she is. Plus she had to work to become what she is. She needed hours of meditation and mind bending. She seems original to me.*)

I cannot hinder my life for the comfort of others. There are too many weak, unrealized people for me ever even to consider that. I would be a slave to the random weakness, and random oppressive opinions, in all people. I would never be such a fool. Nothing matters enough to enslave yourself to anything," Dad. But then came a thought that seemed to speak itself.   "Including me?"   she said riddled with abandonment issues. *She felt traces of the disease still in her. There is often more pettiness to be cleaned up after one transcends "god's" peace.*

"Including me. Including you," the girl felt a discomfort in her belly. She wanted to matter to her father. "It might be hard to hear such things from a father you have never known, but you must not be so arrogant that you would think that you are so important that you must matter. Importance is a lie we give ourselves to feel valuable. We are not valuable. We are equal. Equally nothing important. Just things that take up space in time," Dad. She relaxed the pain in her belly by relaxing the part of her mind that felt that she must be important. The father seemed pleased as he noticed that she did it. "It is rare to find a person that understands me. I am glad it is my daughter.*" We are our own therapists. We need only be honest with ourselves and engulf ourselves in those situations and the mindsets necessary to explore our most fascinating and curious mentalities. People go to therapists only because they cannot be honest enough with themselves to realize how weak and worthless they really are. There are many psychoses, even the one's we choose.* There was no reason for the girl to burden herself with such useless pain. She disposed of it.

The girl decided she was quite tired. So she went to sleep in the house. It was too hot. She pulled the entire bed out of the house. She found that several others had already done this. Her exhaustion carried her into sleep despite the heat.

When she awoke in the morning, first she showered the stickiness away then she wrote down a poem. She thought of the grandfather and the father and the conversations they had.

"We Babbled"

We babbled unto the earth
    with our brilliant lunacy.
Hours lost to babble.
    To philosophical delights.
Endless possibilities.
    For the salvation of ourselves.
We babbled, babbled, babbled,
    To save a world that will never know.
    To free a planet that will never laugh.

From the elder spilt creation.
From the younger spilt devastation.
Love poured from them both,
Like a fountain none would drink.
    No one wanted that disease.
No one wanted the babble curse.

Never listening to the rant.
Many went to sleep or eat.
And the babble lit the night,
    burning both their minds.
Laughter. Babble. Laughter.
The futility of it all.
Laughter. Babble. Laughter.
The game went on and on.
Joy exploded from their hopes
and ever growing dreams.

Laughter. Babble. Laughter.
Forever spilled for God.

God never seems to listen to the great philosophies of earth. Perhaps that is why man made himself god. Perhaps that is why man's ignorance ran away with fear. Perhaps that is where the disease came from.

Chapter 26

Divorium

"What's this?"

"The Divine Sage. It is legal now, but won't be soon. It can be important in breaking the illusion," man.

"Let's smoke it. If I get horny and we have sex, don't ever talk to me about it, please. It may be like it never existed to me."

"Don't worry you won't," laughing man. He packed some into a large chambered water pipe. "You smoke it. You might need outside help. Besides I don't want any," man, "Take in as much as you can. This isn't weed."

She began to smoke it heavily. The smoke burnt her throat, like the memory of a heated poker she once stuck to her skin. Halfway through the third intake of smoke the girl began to laugh. She laughed a laugh in emptiness that echoed into nothingness and struck her deaf. The laughter was all she was, and she wasn't even really that. She was gone. She was void. Nothing of the earth existed. All pain...all suffering...all hope...all love...all eternity...Gone. Completely joyfully gone.

After what she was told was a minute and a half or so she glided out of it. She felt peaceful. She felt like she had in certain states of meditation. She felt void of worry. Empty. Complete. United with anything she saw.

"The best part about this drug is that you can't do it often. Your body won't let you get high every time. It voids dependency. One cannot grow stagnant in it. No slavery," laughing man.

"I like to be reminded here and there that I am not what I sometimes let myself believe I am."

They laugh at the drug induced blurb.

Poem:

"Hi"

To any man a fine life,
Of excitement and experience.
But you grow tired.
It's repetition. It's repetition to you.
You grow frustrated,
Infuriated! You babble to yourself.

You grow further away.
More distant from your reality.
Once so sharp was your mind,
so keen on great fact,
But it drifts in fantasy now.
Unprotected. Unbound.
Temptation to leave.
Leave it all in your past.
The unknown pulls strong at your face.
  You are losing yourself
  in the laughter of your friends.
You appear strong,
but you are man.
  You feel the laughter inside you,
        all about you,
                constantly against you.

She's beautiful. The insanity.
She flirts with your salvation.
For now you resist.
You lay calmly down.
You run to security,
to what you thought you were.

Some is gone. Some is new.
Some is very dark and now dead.
You will drift again from your sobriety,
young child, my man.
When you do,
I'll be here.
I will play with your thoughts.
I will feast on your mind.
I will laugh at your words.
                    I am you, and you are yours too.

Chapter 27

The Escape

The girl sat on the beach drinking a margarita as the sun continued to rise and warm her body. She reveled in the sensation her body felt when she was in a state to notice beauty. ***She knows that feeling that she is in beauty is putting bias to the world. She knows that calling something beautiful or ugly is part of the Dark Society's disease. She knows it can warp her. But she lets it happen, because she knows it cannot take her. And she knows it is beautiful.*** There are consequences to knowing the oneness of the world. It can lose all the joy of definition and bias. The girl knows it is not real. She uses the sensation for her pleasure, as she would use pain for her pleasure. ***If you know all is fake and can have any random bias or definition applied to it. It is yours to love, be it bliss or pain. It can't hurt you, either way. There is never anything to lose.*** And be sure that love can hurt just as much as any suffering pain.

And so she talked in her head. Always putting herself in a true reality check so she didn't get carried away by the game she indulged in.

The girl had noticed lately that the world was gripping her. It was pressing on her again. It felt too real. She jumped at things that she had not previously jumped at. She worried about things that she knew did not matter. She fed on any information that anyone would tell her. She listened so intently to anyone that spoke of anything that could aid her knowledge. She noticed that this lust for knowledge would sweep her away and lose her to the physical world, to the petty weak-man's game. This state is the natural state of her ego. It was powerful. It was brilliant. But most certainly it is a trap. It can be useful, but it must never become the real truth. She noticed that her mind felt that if it kept thinking it would not have to deal with any pain. Silly ego. Why does humankind have such a weak, nearly useless way of dealing with the world? The ego almost seems like a mutation that fear created to deal with the world. Like it is a sort of warped evolution. Perhaps she should take a walk. Maybe the physical sensations of the drugs have been making her identify too much with the physical world.

The girl walked off into a canyon and up over some mountains, and then back down into another canyon, not far from the ranch. As she entered the canyon, she noticed thousands upon thousands of tiny purple butterflies. And the surprise of large piles of sand that had had the bottoms swept away by a flood and so sat like giant mushrooms in a field of myth. Her mind and the minds of so many would think that something like this could not exist. There is no way that such heavy mounds could sit on such tiny pillars of sand. The mounds were six or seven feet wide and rose up a good five feet over her head, and the pillars they rested on were only two feet wide, maybe. Amazing. But it was true. The girl was happy that she wasn't on any narcotics so that she could feel the realism of the physical surrealism. She sat, and marveled.
She closed her eyes. She had felt nothing before and this is bliss. How many times had she thought that she had some of it? Stillness. Ahhh. It felt good. It felt good only in the way that nothing can feel good. It felt deeper. It felt like the deepest. And always there is difference to feel in the nothing. Always remain humble. Always believe that you are neither strong nor weak. You can gain techniques, such as levitation, but they mean nothing. Nothing can ever truly be conquered or built. Nothing that man can create can remain. ***The mind jumps and never notices.***

She stared at the greenish desert trees around her. She looked down to the notebook cover that held her poetry. The cover had faded much. The leaves never fade. The rocks or dirt never fade. Nothing that existed before man thought that he could make a world ever fades. It can change some color, but it never loses its true pigment. Like a sunburned arm can be red, but it still holds its pigment and the normal color returns shortly. If any manmade creation is left in the sun, it can be completely bleached over time. Arrogant, childish man. So blinded by their own lies of importance. *Often the same thoughts of things are applied over and over to different situations, developing deeper understanding of her own philosophies. Always it was different to her.*

The girl laughed. She felt blessed to be in such a situation, even though logically feeling blessed made no sense. Nothing can be more blessed than anything else. The randomness of lying sensations just let us think we are. She rode her thoughts. She rode them to this thought: She chose to feel blessed. Others in that situation may feel the agony of the grueling hike or the sting of the cactus she fell into. But silly her, she felt blessed. She laughed at the landscape that shouldn't exist. She laughed at herself. *It is funny how our attitudes perceive the world exactly as we imagine it. Be a person negative or positive or any degree in between, we make everything a certain way, and we never even notice it.* We never notice the control we actually have when we let ourselves lose the control of having to perceive something a certain way that we have been programmed with.

The mind skipped through the thoughts that explained the world in philosophical poetry. By now she knew again that this was not silence. She knew the mind needed more meditation than this hike. But at least it was placed in check. She needed that. She re-felt her center on things around her. *She is strong enough to let the mind grip her and not lose control.*
Perhaps a poem:

"The Mountain's Peace"

Within the trees and shaded sun,
where life is full in faith,
I laid my head upon a rock,
so soft I nearly slept.
It is good to find the lull, just now.
A moment of empty peace.
A chance to breathe a breath…
…a breath in purity.

The forest sings me to ease.
I whisper her my thanks.
As her creatures crawl about me,
I simply let them be.
I rest within the silence,
which has haunted me before..
but today even silence rests,
and I thank her for that gift.

Yet within a blissful haze
I remembered I was bleeding.
My hand went to the wound.
I lost myself to peace.
As I faded off to sleep,
I thanked the one who'd shot me…
I thanked him for the gift.

Chapter 28

The Lie of Love

The girl decided to take a trip away from the ranch for a while. She began to meditate a great deal. The physical happenings of the world slowed the frantic pace her mind had been putting to it. She eased out a large amount of fear that the ego exploded upon her. She was open and understanding. She had no need to force herself on anyone. She had no need to hate. It was too much work to hate. It was the perfect time for someone to invade her.

Through some light conversation she stumbled into a relationship with some boy. She allowed herself to move deeply for him. She felt sensations of dizzying excitement. She felt her bones ache with love. She felt the deep sensations that she always wanted to feel. She felt no coldness. She felt only oneness, completeness. She wanted to be with this boy. She wanted only his cock to be inside of her. She absorbed his every essence. She felt that she was his eternity. And he told her all the same. Her emotions were at their height. She would often cry out of pure joy or pure sadness.

Time ceased in this love. Time died. She would never be able to exactly recall when or for how long it lasted. But she remembers the pain she felt, the death she felt when he told her that they were so different. He told that girl that he grew bored with her. Her passion meant nothing. He had fucked other girls. She was not ever to be a wife to him...And she had thought that she already was. She wept with tears of agonizing madness. She did not weep because she lost the liar. She did not weep because of the hypocrisy that appeared. She did not weep for her own ignorance that did not see that they were so different. She wept because she could not set him free from the trap that he was in. She could not save him from his ego that exploded with deceit.

It does not matter what the lies were exactly. It matters that he could not see it. It matters that she could not save this one person. It was the same old agony she had always felt. She let him in so deep with the blind trust that the holy have. She told such pure truths under midnight skies. And it was not enough to free him from his ego that crushed hers. How could she have been thinking that she could save a world? How could she think that she was a type of hero *(even if she wasn't attached to the heroism.)*? She told to him deep truths of freedom and they meant nothing. He could not understand them. The lies that he could understand only served as a catalyst for her to open herself more. The lies of understanding. It made her more vulnerable. It made her program herself more with his significance and his identity and the love that she believed in.

And for all the glorious progress that she made at the time she met this man, she had an explosion of her own ego at the end. The ego exploded to protect the carnated girl, to distract her from the emotional pain that could kill her. Much time seemed to pass before she could let herself be vulnerable to herself again. It was hard to see herself completely honestly. With an ego explosion, years of accumulated truth can be clouded. But she fought through it quicker than most ever had.

She learned one great lesson from the "epic love." She learned that all love, all hate, everything that we long for, we have full control over. We grant "true love" to ourselves. We create it because we want it. She had thought this before. But she did not understand it. She had conquered aspects of this control in herself before, but she clung to other aspects or the illusions. *That is how it is. There is no hypocrisy in it. To dismantle the walls of the ego, we must take it down one brick at a time. And we must move from section to section. And when the wall falls in upon itself we must clean away the clutter and continue our task. Sometimes we will turn around and notice the wall is rebuilt where it should have been destroyed.* She learned that he invaded her at the exact random time in her life for it to happen. She learned much from the pain. She learned that she is far stronger than she thought she was. The girl began to actually understand, through severe experience, the philosophies she is.

Like all things of her life this event made her notice the wonderment that she naturally is. *She despises the humanness that is her main tool in making her divine. The positive path cut its way once more. There is a clear delineation between the negative path and the positive path, even if they are both beyond good and evil, they are different. They make your life clearly one thing or another thing. Within the goodness of internal peace there really is little way to choose the negative. If the path is true even the noticeably horrible will be good.* Throughout the time that she tried to love with the full joy of the ego, she never tried to be negative. She tried only to have no fear, only to bring love, only to bare everything. By having no fear she was naturally positive, be it in creation or destruction. It is why the girl only saw the similarities in relationships. The exact similarities of every single soul. Differences didn't matter. She suffered by her sadness, but it wasn't "bad." She noticed that her very life is the example and the proof that fear is the only truly negative and possibly evil-like thing in all of existence. She returned again to the ranch. She had nowhere else to be.

Chapter 29

Old and Tired

She awoke to the yellow morning light. She had slept on the beach again, under a palapa. She looked at a watch that someone had given her. Twelve hours. She had slept for twelve hours. Sleep consumes her these days. She looked to her left and saw a dog. The dog was asleep. Animals sleep a lot. They don't care. They don't have this bizarre programming of having to do something. They never have to do anything. That lie must have come from some tyrant or coward far in the past that had to build a society to feel safe. The girl had heard of a school of Taoism whose disciples only sleep when they are tired, and at no set time. Entire cultures exist that defy programming, that defy fear, but the Dark Society uses the fear as a breeder of power, over and over. The Dark Society always rang through her head. Again and again. An echo of what she had to do. She always new. She stared out to the ocean...and in her was that sensation that she had to do something. She knows freedom, she knows bliss, she knows how to have it, but she will give it up for the world, to stop the Dark Society. ***It is the most noble of lives.***

As she stared out to the sea and through her mind and herself, she noticed a song in her head. So often there was a song in her head. Something she could have heard anywhere for any reason. It cycled through a great selection and at total random spun it, not for amusement, but just to have something playing. She tried to silence it. The fully orchestrated, perfectly duplicated music is harder to silence than thought. It comes from a different area of the brain. In meditation she must always focus on it separately. It takes more time to relax into silence. The mind is an annoyance to those that must continue to use it for their sacrifice

after having known the peace of silence. It is easier to stay in shape than to have to keep getting into shape every time toning is needed. But the sloth and the pain of letting the mind run rampant was holy and astounding for her quest. To affect this world she had to use her mind and her ego. No one will ever know her sacrifice. Nothing can understand but her. ***So brave. So lonely.***
So deeply impressive.

True cause has no origin of a traumatic event. There is no desperado that shot down the wife of some random hero. True cause is simply what the hero is. The girl is the cause of freedom.

Chapter 30

Anger Swells

She awoke suddenly. Nightmares. A series of them. She had had nightmares before, but none like these. It wasn't what was happening in the dreams, it was how they made her feel. She had experienced much pain in her life. She had seen much death. She had dreamt about these great adventures without fear. She had imagined great adventures in her dreams that were plagued with threat to her life and the people around her, but she had felt no fear or anxiety from the dreams. She felt anxiety. She felt fear. It was horrible. The girl thought how sad it is, and how difficult it must be for the weak to feel such pain in so many circumstances. One dream was of tiny creatures trying to eat her. Another of a woman being filleted with a machete over a waterfall. Both acts she knew should not have brought her such fear. The girl knew that she should not be touched by them. Why was she? What was trying to be told from the depths of her subconscious? Is she supposed to be more compassionate towards those suffering? No. That doesn't make sense. They can stop suffering if they simply choose to. If they let go of it. Is she full of instinctual fears of pain that are surfacing? Is she supposed to be doing something now? Perhaps, that is it. There is no better way for a deeper knowledge to tell her something than to give her the jolt of fear that should not even exist within her. But what? What has she been thinking about lately? The anger of the war.

Conversations often appear in her mind with no forward or introduction to the event or the characters. Certain things touch her and move her. Do we have to figure out why?

"What war are you talking about?" Gringo, "There is no war."

"People must choose to make wars."

"This isn't the middle ages," Gringo.

"What?! All ages are the same. There is someone who realizes that something does not have to be a certain way. We do not have to believe someone else's lies. Someone or group of someones had to create a code of chivalry, knights didn't just exist. Rome, the cowboy way of freedom, all times that the slaves wish they lived in, came about because someone made the time that. People hardened themselves. Do you think the break away from the great provider of Britain was easy for a starving America? Do you think it was comfortable. No. It was fricking horrible. They gave up their lives, their wealth, their power, for an idea they knew they would never see. To an idea they saw fail before they even died. That is real heroism. That is philosophical holiness."

"Why make a war? That is ignorant. War is not a good thing," Gringo.

"War is an amazingly fun thing, if you are not a cowardly slave. I could bash your head into this brick walkway until you are a useful human being. By "useful" I mean, so that something could eat your dead body. But anyway I don't feel like it, so I am not going to."

"What the hell is wrong with you. You don't know what war is! You don't know what freedom is either!" Gringo.

"Why is the slave mind so void of logic? Why is this conversation always the same with every wretch I meet? Why does the slave always assume that they know everything about somebody just by seeing them once? Shut up! It is because they see people through the lies that they see themselves through. Through the lies of a person that they do not know. Now, this conversation is over. I suggest that you prepare yourself to die, if you don't want to die in the war that I am creating I suggest you get away from it." She begins to walk away.

"Wait I am not done. You are an idiot!" Gringo.

"Slave. Listen. Why do you think you have to be right?"

"I don't, but apparently you do!" Gringo.

She shakes her head. She turns and walks away. Why do they always keep talking?

Something is nagging her. ***Her mind drifts in its games.*** The war. The war. That's right the war. What first? A great book to inspire people before and after the war? A great movie? Or just war? ***After it is known that the girl is dead will she be remembered as immaculate or holy...the girl should be remembered as logical. The girl only evaluated and deduced the simple structure of human thought and interpretation. And so she warped herself and warped anyone else she wanted too. Will anyone see the subtleties?***

The war. Why is it in the girl? Why is it the way? It will be done.

Chapter 31

To Be Stabbed

As he violently penetrated her, she witnessed the difference in sexual mindset between man and woman. It is always so powerful and often void of emotion for a man. It is often such a surrender to many girls that she had watched being screwed. How interesting. The reason is simple. It is so random that she hadn't thought of it before. He is a stabber of something. While she must be stabbed. The woman personifies herself subconsciously as a victim of something. The man is a killer of something. In the animal kingdom the man always attacks and the woman always tries to avoid it, for a short while. She thought of that as she watched two pigeons in the distance trying to mate. It is so obvious. And amazing. A woman invites a man to stab her. To enter into her. The submission is amazing. Although many women have also detached themselves from the stabbing and only crave the sensation, but it is usually more of a blocking out of emotion, rather than a transcending. Perhaps this is why gay men are more sensitive and oftentimes more vulnerable. They too, are stabbed. Perhaps it is this carnal ordeal that makes many women identify with caring gay men. ***There is so much debauchery hidden in simple actions.*** Even those enlightened straight men that have discovered the glorious male clit tucked deep into the anus, named the prostate, seem gentled and more understanding of death and difference. ***Such a deep part of the disease is hidden away in sexual inhibition and the lack of exploration into the pleasure of all sex. If one cannot look at their sexual depths, one cannot look at their soul. Sex is part of the ego that must be accepted and opened into vulnerability and bliss to be freed from the disease that is fear of being our natural, dirty, constantly vulnerable selves.*** She looked at his face as he jabbed her. She saw the rage in him that was needed to ejaculate. Only the free can be easeful and loving, but still, of course, enjoy the carnal dream of violent raping sex. *She certainly does.* What is that like? Quickly she overturned his body with the tool of him not expecting strength and grabbed a knife that was set on his pair of jeans. She stabbed into him again and again. She gazed at the look on his face with determined study. Why isn't he enjoying this? Why can't he invite the stabbing? She had. Sure it doesn't feel like a penis and a vagina, but why live by that stereotype that stab wounds can't feel good. *A free man loves pain and pleasure. When in pain, let yourself enjoy it. Don't believe that it is bad.* After he was dead from shock, not blood loss, she stabbed for a time watching blood patterns spurt forth artistic insight. She understands man more greatly now. She feels relaxed. Man sex feels good. Well, the base egoic psychology of it anyway. *The struggle in the mind when understanding is reached is chaotic, unhindered, and violent*

What makes her separate from what a man is anyway? This hole in her? Men have holes in them. Her specially designed hole? This bleeding pulsing wound that sheds death from itself once a month in a rotting stench filled rejection? This pussy? It is a disgusting thing. It is as disgusting as a throbbing, expanded blood filled rod that shoots sticky, sharply tasting microscopic parasitic organisms designed to invade a body, her body. *Accept the disgustingness you are. Don't try to pretend it is something else. Don't lie.* These are bodies, made to breed, and breed pleasurably (oddly,
original enough). They work in their given way. They are disgusting. They are different. They are everything people hate if they didn't happen to be on them specifically. In actuality, we, man and woman, boy and girl, are separated by nothing. If we all brought forth the spiritual beauty that is the same in us all, there would be no distinction between man and woman. The funny thing about that is that the species might die out if that happens. Man would fuck what it wanted. Woman would fuck what it wanted. It might not have to be each other. There is a physical way the world exists. It may exist all around us in any way, but to maintain itself it must work in a certain way. Sperm for an egg. That is, if you want a creature to rip itself from your body after it had lived as a parasite in your be ly. (Precious isn't it.)

The girl can be anything she wants to be. Why not a boy? Why not let her think of herself like that? The body is nothing. The mind is nothing. Her little pussy is pointless. It is as pointless as the propagation of this diseased species. Make yourself anything, and what is important can still never really change. She cannot change the ultimate truth of her demise and the purity of her spirit, but in this world...she can do anything...at least within herself.

Chapter 32

High Chatter

The mind chatters away to find a conclusion to this world. It finds a way to play the game as we choose to dream it. The boy *(girl)* thinks on the Buddha. **She notices that she can more exactly observe herself. She can observe her physical world, her mental world, even her subconscious world, all from her "spiritual" world.** The Buddha is nothing but a distraction of false enlightenment. One cannot overcome the egoic world by focusing so intently on a part of it, alive or dead. To focus on the Buddha is to separate yourself from yourself with a simple inflection of the mind. To be absorbed into any worship of anything is a distraction from the observation of the self. The mind can trick you. It does it all the time. The nose thinks that a smell is seamen, but it is not seamen, it is bleach. It has happened to the boy *(girl)* before. To become the power that we are, we must reject the Buddha, as we must reject our own senses. We must reject the logic that is pinned on us by the ego (including and especially the mind). The boy *(girl)* feels love for the Buddha. He *(she)* feels adoration for his quest, but be sure that there is a vast difference between adoration and worship. The Buddha knew this. The Buddha rejected everything. The Buddha rejected the Brahman path. Just as Jesus did, when he went to India to study a nameless type of religion that he dreamt to change Judaism into, but the Jews mangled his dream with the ego and became Christian worshipers like they did with Abraham, like the future Buddhists did, like the future Muslims and Islamics did, like they all always do in the same old boring trap that they think they invented anew for some new god. If one searches for truth with any desire of physical body of physical mind they will find only the physical body and the physical mind, no truth. Only illusions that try to fill the void of not mattering.

We must accept that we do not matter. Only then will we find anything of any worth. Why try to save a world that will not understand? Why not? ***What else is she doing?***

How was he *(she)* driving the car? He *(she)* doesn't remember anything of the road for the past twenty or thirty miles. Obviously the mind is not needed to drive. The mind is not needed to function in the physical world. Something else can drive the car. How could he *(she)* know that a turn is coming up? How could he *(she)* know where the lines on the road are? He *(she)* knows because the range of true consciousness extends beyond the confines of the body. There is proof for it everyday in so many actions. The less we focus on the body and the mind, the more we can feel it. He *(she)* focused on the area around the speeding car. Every fraction of the consciousness he *(she)* knew so deeply, he *(she)* could realize filled a cubed area around the car. His *(her)* flesh tingled. He *(she)* wanted to close his *(her)* eyes, but the full faith was not there to do it. ***Still there is a sense of protecting the body, which is certainly hard to escape while retaining the courage to interact in the physical world.*** But why would consciousness be limited to a certain area around him *(her)*? It is arrogant, and so egoic, to think that consciousness can only be extended to a limited area from a center that we call "our" body. But will he *(she)* leave his *(her)* body if he *(she)* extends beyond the center of his *(her)* universe, his *(her)* body. There is still fear. Will it ever end? Let go. Let go. There is an ache in his *(her)* bones. But ease the body. It can't be forced. It can be let go, relaxed, but the faith is not yet there to have the courage to relax it fully. ***He (she) doesn't want the game to end yet. Want can be a tricky thing to deal with. Can you see why the chosen path of balance is so difficult? What madness the struggle for balance breeds in a brilliant mind that can understand so much. There are two truths. A spiritual one and an egoic one. The knowledge that she cannot die and the knowledge that her body will die. She doesn't want to kill the others in the car either. Are we game masters or are we pawns? Probably neither.***

The chatter in the mind the marijuana creates is deafening. Too much drugs send the mind out of control. It is fun to think, but we cannot be ruled by thought.

We cannot be ruled by drugs. The best advantage to marijuana is that it can bring up more latent pieces of chatter and fear that the spirit can deal with and put in check for the ego. It can help us deconstruct ourselves by over-constructing our super ego and our subconscious. It inflames the mind, and so it inflames the ego. It makes it more observable.

Chapter 33

Sight Beyond Sight

On the ranch...in the dirt...he *(she)* found a tarantula. He *(she)* tried to edge it into a cup with her finger. In less than a flash, the spider rapped itself around his *(her)* finger. His *(her)* eyes did not witness the event because it happened to fast for them to be used. In an instant his *(her)* mind transferred consciousness to his *(her)* finger. There was a fully detailed vision of what the spider looked like in his *(her)* consciousness even though his *(her)* eyes could not see it. **The Third Eye? A less used eye anyway**. He *(she)* flung it off his *(her)* hand. People around him *(her)* were laughing. They thought he *(she)* jumped. They thought he *(she)* was afraid. But there was no welling or surge of fear. Only reaction. Only a slow and logical conclusion that warped time and took place in the instant of that steady instinct when what must be done is done, and the human body is preserved.   In the flash of the action it felt as if time slowed. Time was certainly warped for his *(her)* purposes. He *(she)* logically thought out a plan of action in a time of action that was so quick no one even saw. Everyone that was laughing only thought the spider backed up and made him *(her)* jump. She *(a lapse in the new identity)* explained nothing. No one would understand what occurred. No one she knows can observe themselves so precisely, so fully in understanding of what the subconscious and conscious minds had to do to interact.

The war. The war. The war. The war. The war.
Stop it! Stop it. He *(she)* knows. **She almost thought "I". The cause is so ingrained in her chosen purpose of life that it melds into her truth of reality. Imagine what it is like to know that nothing matters, to know that deeply**

throughout all of your being, yet for some 'god'-fucked reason you are a creature of unbending destiny. You know you are an important key, but you don't believe in importance. Again the duel reality. The balance and the control it takes to control the subtleties can only be achieved when you do not care about having control. Only then can you let go enough from the lies of the Dark Society that tell you that the ego controls. One can be able to control the superego, the subconscious and the ego from a point of "higher" reality. In the contradictions, in what the mind says does not make sense, are the answers. If a human ego transcends enough, it can use the mind with detachment from taught logic and let the mind understand what should be illogical to it. It is possible, ask an Astral Physicist. What is true does not always make sense, especially to the majority who were never taught to think in the first place. So far beyond is the concept to think beyond thought itself. The true spiritualists and the great scientists are entering into a new realm of thinking, that which is beyond the programming of the planet, beyond what is naturally needed to survive, this is because we do not need to survive anymore because of society. The Dark Society has advantages for us all, even me, even her, even for those who have yet to come. Since everything a human being knows is first warped and created through initial contact and initial feeling and warped further by influences of time and cause, and we can observe this, and we can see how their perceptions are effecting all things within six degrees, we can discover the way to change and we can choose to warp ourselves by simply choosing to perceive something differently. Hence the ability to create egoic words to attempt to explain a randomly chosen girl's existence as a god. The mind can invent new logic from whichever tool of various human reality (ego, subconscious, etc.) it chooses to use.

Maybe the boy *(girl)* is a schizophrenic. The duel reality of understanding may be schizophrenia. The boy *(girl)* talks to himself *(herself)* all the time. The constant debate against logic is certainly not normal, not to this extent. But what does it matter whether the boy *(girl)* believes it or not, the life will play out anyway. Maybe as it had to. It is important to be able to tell what part of human existence the logic is coming from. What part is using the mind. There are many ways to reason. The technique of faith can be used to know that the mindless path *(the superego (and beyond that))* is the only unbiased observer of the self. He *(she)* quieted the doubt. His *(her)* faith is strong, but he *(she)* wants it stronger.

Chapter 34

Calamus Thought

Man. Man. Boy. Woman. Screams in the skull. Humankind. It tears at her. Was all the meditation only a self-medication to stop the pain of thought? It couldn't have been. Is it more painful now because she has felt the relativity of silence. Is this normal? His *(Her)* path seems sacred. It's hard. No. It must be true. The meditations must be true. He *(She)* felt the nothingness in the water when he *(she)* was young and was only first realizing. He *(She)* must silence the mind to cope with the ego that is necessary for him *(her)* to develop to offer salvation to the world. The Glorification of Humankind. A lie. A lie. Man is not the god he imagines. Once they thought the universe revolved around the Earth. The attitude has not changed. The lie only has different words. Many still think that animals have no thought when clearly they react logically to situations. At the ranch much wildlife eat the grasses under the cover of night, they only run when the lights from a car shine upon them. They know that they are only seen in the light. They know that man is their enemy. They can identify an enemy. To say that animals have no deduction is to say that wretched peasants have no deduction. It is the same god complex that the Jews and Christians enslaved millions with. That's not the point though. That's not the point. The point is that man is not a god in any way. Man is a parasite. Maybe an ameba. Think of stars and how they are laid out. Planets rotating around a sun, held by gravity. How is the sun held there? Gravity, rotation in orbit. It is proof of a center to the universe. The sun must move, like the protons around a nucleus, like people around the Earth. Although gravity can be partially broken and ego can be overcome, the universe was once bound by, for lack of a better word, design or happenstance. But why? And how did man become so weak and afraid that he had to run from the world under the guise of becoming a god and so creating societies and shelters, be they houses or religions, to protect itself. How did man believe that he was not a parasite or an ameba and that he should be more than what he is? In the beginning there was only silence. There was only nothing. And so, there was truth.   But man began to speak. Now there are lies, massive layers of lies to cover truths about what we really are.   Lies that cover insecurities, insecurities that cover fear, fear that covers the truth about our nothingness, about our vastness. Man must be stopped. And only man knows what man is doing. Only man can stop man. Only man understands the dark path. Only man can travel the Dark Path. Only a man can be the destroyer. The Freer. The Liberator. ***The voices strike out from her mind in fury that will not silence.*** The boy *(girl)* will not take calamus root again. ***She could not silence the drug induced talk in her head. She could not hush the madness of the mind. She had to simply accept it and ride it out. Believing it would end. Meditation can not save her. And so she has further proof that the mind is not what we are. It is not the greatest knower. It is not where truth can be found. It is a device that she wants to overcome, just as the body is, just as the universe is. Her god complex exists, but one must see that hers is not from fear and lies, but from humility and rational contemplation, from the vastness of understanding. Her complex has different results, because it is different than yours. She has never ran from the truth, even when the truth told her that she will not matter, that she is nothing, and that the freedom fighter is a slave to truth. There is more to understand in the universe and it is not understood by putting it under a microscope. It is understood by silently and honestly looking into our own godless spirits.***

Chapter 35

Learned

She teaches me. I become more like her. Why me? Is it because I rejected so much? Is it that strength that she saw in me? Oh, little girl, I am understanding your free madness, but only by flowing through you, into you...only by experiencing you having the memories you know.
The girl *(She has stopped identifying herself with man or woman, so becomes "girl" again for easier physical identification.) (I notice that I am using "I" a lot. My ego is fighting to stay separate from hers. I must let go. I must not be afraid of losing myself. I must speak "I" and have it identify nothing but an object that is this body.)*

She has been learning techniques. She is always suddenly surprised by what she is learning. She is surprised at the knowledge she has gained. It is hard for her to remember where the knowledge came from. She often just has it. Much of it grows from herself, rather than from someone else. Knowledge slowly swells from her spirit, like a spring slowly drowning her back to death. For the majority of the knowledge she seeks is already in her. It only waits to be interpreted by the spirit so that the mind can rationalize it and so the ego can use it, which will let the body overcome its weaknesses. She can find it by simply paying attention to herself, like all true knowledge. But the knowledge she has been gaining as of the current flash is not true knowledge, but physical knowledge with physical techniques. It is often faster to simply be taught the physical techniques, like hand to hand combat, but even still she has an instinct for it, which flows only from the depths of true knowledge. A place where fear and lies are fought. She learns of the simple world of explosives. She learns the art of killing. She has often noted to herself how simple it is to kill. How simple it is to stop the world's disease. Man is so blinded with fear that he never realizes the fragility of his self on Earth. Cowardly human. Naive human. If man should fear anything, with any amount of egoic rational, man should fear himself. At any random point his mind could snap with any release of any random chemical that he naturally produces, and he could bludgeon his fist into his own throat. Again and again. Wouldn't that make it easier, if the disease regulated itself. But alas, a young girl must sacrifice her soul because human reality is too weak. Murderers.

Oftentimes she contemplates the peaceful means to war. From boycotts, to fastings, to speeches of swaying emotion. It is her preference, but logic always leads back to violence. It has spread beyond the reaches of physical peace. People do not have the courage nor the strength to conquer themselves. It doesn't matter what glorious words of freedom flow into their ears, they will manipulate it and warp it through the filter of fear. And every true word of love will only meet with shallowness and lies. Often she has dreamt of another, one person that could save the world from her. One that could show the girl unhindered love, not so she could have it, but so she could be amongst it. But then would come, or she would hear, of another encounter with some policing force that would blindly inflict the fears of some district attorney or some attorney general. She would hear of lies used to exploit more power from a people so confounded with the everyday stress of living in a culture where the specialization of a job so deeply distracts people with a lust for growing perfection and securing of minute power and comfort that they do not even have a second to stop and see what is being done to them. So they pay their taxes, blindly, to give power to those that would suck out from their dark lives every ounce of freedom that they are blessed with the opportunity of having from the second of their birth and infinite spiritual equality. But they would rather not think of the oppressors. They would rather think of what is comfortable to them right at the flashing second and the fleeting seconds that they covet so foolishly. Wouldn't it be a heavenly step in their lying utopiotic societies if they prescreened the disease from those they elect to serve them with years of meditation and self-inflection? Well, supposedly. The war is emanate.

Potassium Chlorate and petroleum jelly. It is all she has seen for days. The tediousness lets her mind meditate on thought. It dances furiously through genius while recording her every action in a place she will never need to release into conscious memory. A place where repetition sits. First she smashes the potassium chlorate (found from a fireworks supply company. *Sub-Thought.*) with a rolling pin, then it is mixed with common petroleum jelly for bricking, then slowly, and at a low temperature, it is baked. Fifty gallon drums are beginning to collect around the ranch. They will be filled with the simple method that the hero McVeigh used to defend his holy heart in response to the slaughter of all he had loved from Waco in Oklahoma, fertilizer and diesel fuel. ***Brave men fight giants so that they may be called devils.*** Simple, with huge results, but harder to transport than her little, cheap, C-4 mixture of baby lube and nutritional supplement.

Peace. Peace. What about peace? Should she just sit and transcend the world and not let the Dark Society effect her? Should she avoid the conflict that makes her feel so inferior from time to time. She feels part of her vengeance is from the ego. She feels it. It pains her. She always goes deeper into herself. But unlike most who go deeper, she is not brought more into non-violence and pacifism, but instead more into war. She realizes the violence that cannot be avoided in this world as she tears through everything she was told to be real by the Dark Society. She grows less flinching as she conquers the insecurities in herself. She grows more sure that she cannot be damned nor saved by any thing. She knows that nothing can be inflicted upon her or granted to her. She grows more at peace with war, with all the non-important death that is all around her. Inflicted by the very existence of life. From a black hole to a meteor to a virus to a jackal to a human to a cancer, all made to live and to kill. It is not killing we must stop. It is the in others will be their own business. fear of being killed that we must stop. The fear

Chapter 36

Death of the Familiar

And so comes something else that seemingly contradicts something else. But do not think with your biases. Think without them, like her. So you may think of everything. So you may experience everything. Only then can you master the qualities of the inherent reflex that the Ninja theories of strength are based on.

Sid is dead. ***She hadn't even fully realized that she had been talking to him lately.*** Had it been so long? Had it been so long since she let herself feel anything? There was never anyone so pure as him, so non-judging, so loving. So real. ***Though stricken with logic and contempt like she is. And so hated and hidden and naturally violent and free---like she is. Her friend just hid it differently.*** He was living a normal life, helping her, but from within the society. He often served as an alibi to her "crimes" against the Dark Society. She had committed many. She had committed crimes against life, against her friend. He was the only one that had not betrayed her internally, and so she never felt like she had to protect her holy path and betray him by keeping him from anything, be it physical, mental, or important. He never held back anything that she asked. He realized that she offered herself as a sacrifice for the peace of the world. She loved him. She loved the purity of what he understood. She loved how Sid understood her. And so she let the sadness overtake her. She appeared to herself at a funeral. She saw the scars where the lumps had been removed from his neck. She fell to her knees and wept. She wept with the rawest of power. With pure energy. She wept with the sadness of such massive intensity that she bellowed. She cried out. She shook and she yelled. She wept for death itself.

She wept for all human connection that she felt for all humankind. She wept with the rage that it takes to be willing to destroy a planet. She wept with the real power of the soul. She shattered her entire existence and relation to the world in the bliss of her absorption into sadness. She thought in her tears that she knows death to be nothing. She <u>knows</u> it. She knows from direct experience. The only way to know anything. So why does she feel it? Is it so ingrained in the human experience to feel sadness like this? To feel Death? She began to view herself from without. She journeyed to the point in herself where she could see with non-attachment and she observed herself crying. But soon she subsided. Her bawling eased. From non-attachment there was no need to weep. The emotion fell away as it became all she felt. She felt it deeply. As she felt it, she came only back to herself. She came only back to the silence that exists when there is nothing to be attached to, nothing to own the human self or to control it. One must feel the emotion. They must be consumed to understand it. To let the lies of what the common emotion should be...fall away. She let the badness of the sadness fall away. It became unnecessary. The sensation of epic pain and failure and yearning became only an experience. And she began to enjoy and appreciate it without bias. She exploded with laughter. She laughed deeply. She laughed knowing that Sid would laugh if he had any kind of continuing attachment to the illusion of human reality. And so there is the punch-line to the cosmic joke. The joke is herself, and how seriously she can take herself. She is so unbelievably unimportant. Good Journey Sid.

Thank you for choosing to live until you had no choice but to expand.

Chapter 37

So Enters the Next of Them—Zarat

The girl sat and stared into the sand. So randomly and perfectly carved were the tiny pieces of smoothed rock. There must be some sort of mathematical layout for their shapes. Of course, there must be, it can be reproduced on a computer. All physical reality is so base, formulaic, and highly decodable.

"It is funny how it is growing," man.

Pulled from her thought, *it always takes her a minute to be able to communicate in words again,* "What."

"There are a lot of people at the Ranch," Dad.

"Oh, ya, I guess there are."

"This man wants to meet you. His name is Zarat," Dad.

"Hi."

"Can I sit with you?" Zarat.

"Yes."

"How do I deal with pain?" Zarat.

"Do you always ask random strangers bizarre questions?"

"No. Just the ones with bizarre answers," Zarat.

"Put out your arm."

Zarat put out his arm without doubt of what the girl was to show him.

"Prepare your mind to receive pain. If your mind is ready for pain it always hurts less. You do not know where or how it is about to happen, but pain is coming."

Zarat's mind prepared his body with no effort from himself. He tried to do it, but he had already done it. The girl knew that.

The girl laughed slightly to herself as she realized that she had sharpened two fingernails just a day before.

She contemplated in a flash if she was meant to have sharpened them, or if she had just been fortunate. By the time she was finished contemplating she had already sunk her claws into the new person. She stared at him. He grimaced. "Stop. Accept the pain. Accept it. Feel it. Stop thinking about it, and feel it. Just feel it. Can you feel that?" His face eased in expression. "Yes. That's right. Forget that pain hurts. Forget that it is bad." His face winced for a moment as he applied bad to the pain, but quickly he let it go. "Funny, huh. By this point your arm is probably growing a little cold. You know all you need to know. My touch is almost numb to you. Isn't it? Now you know that pain is a lie. You are only used to feeling some way. And this "pain" is not what you are used to. So you let yourself grow used to it. You don't want to believe it, but pain was made up by liars that want to control you. It was made so that you would be afraid of it, and so people can control you with it. Overcome the fear of pain. Accept it as a random experience that can be easily controlled and released, and you need bend to no one's will. It is a secret of all revolution."

She released her grip and looked down to the blood trapped in the cuts on his arm. Pain always looks different when the giver and the taker of pain have accepted it. Pain is not appalling when there is no fear associated with it by the giver or the receiver.
"Thank you," Zarat, "It was worth quitting my job to come here."
"Oh ya, that's horrible."
"What is?" Zarat.
"People in that Dark Society are slaves. I can't imagine having to go to work everyday. Day in and day out. To make someone else money. Some people do it because they love the comfort. They love what that slavery provides them with. They think it is a fair trade to have a game system or a DSL connection. It is nice to have things like that, I can see that, I have fun with them, but not for the cost of that slavery. There are more creative ways to do things. The very sad part about al of it is that people that choose to live in that society must continue to do it. They must not for simple luxury, but for simple survival. Food and such you can

still find relatively cheap, and some charity is always giving it away, but they must continue because of the obscene price of property. It is rent and the price of land that imprison people. Do you know that?"

"Yes. It was Locke that said the essentials to freedom are "Life, Liberty, and Property" and to deny a person a place, a space, to exist is a horrible thing. It is the key to the trap of that society," Zarat.

"Right. The disgusting part is that people take it. They don't realize that the only thing to stand between oppression and freedom is themselves. But most people will accept the slavery, in exchange for the comfort of not having to think. It is a diseased place. And so we come in and we will destroy their security structure and they will hate us, but they will have to face freedom. They will have to be strong, beautiful and humble. There is a small group of people that own a great deal of property and this is not the way. These people should let it go, they should own nothing. Let people give their lands away. Let people live. Let people sell their goods and services, but never should anyone sell land. It is one of the larger hindrances to freedom. Think of how much property is available that some governmental land management organization controls, covets, holds for its own power. And when someone uses that land for farming, even livestock (if you like imprisoning other things), they take your crops, your cattle, and they sell it. They profit from it. Wherever there is any profit by a government, that is a place to apply war. And it is designed to get only more expensive. Real Estate must be sold higher and higher to make profit. The system is designed to destroy itself. Eventually no one will be able to have anything without being a slave. And that is what many people want. The many that profit from the exploitation of the lazy and weak. The world must be reshaped."

"Do you often explode in a flurry of philosophy to people you do not know?" Zarat.

"Yes."

"Oh," Zarat.

"Want to learn how to make a bomb Zarat?"

She felt a clinging to him. He is like Sid to her, but steadier. He believes. But she senses a different effect on her life from this named man.

"That sounds fun," Zarat.

"There's a lot of fun to be had in the world. We just can't be afraid of that pain bullshit you wondered about."
"Why do people flock to you?" Zarat.
"Everyone sees their self in me. No matter what I am doing. That is because I portray my true self. My deep self. My honest self. That which never dies. And everyone has that in common. Everyone has it in them. So they cling to it. It would not have mattered what I chose to do in life, I would have succeeded in some way. Also I do not care that they are there. They never had to come and my war would still be the same. Still I would have succeeded. This war is for fun. The true war is always only within your self. Only within me. Only in the human heart. In life you must accept the fact that you will never actually win. Someone will think differently than you and will come along and fuck it up. Devastate your holy plan. In life, you will lose, no matter what. Accept that, little Zarat, and you have another key to revolution. And a great key to truth."

Poetry...

"Power and Glory"
Series V
Part I

Glory stood in the sun.
His golden armor gleamed.
A hero for the people.
They cheered.
Power stood silently behind him.
Glory smiled wide for the masses.
Power stood glaring behind him.
Power's hand rested firm upon Glory's shoulder.
Glory stepped off the balcony, backwards into the room,
holding his dancing eyes upon the crowd,
until shadow fell upon his face.

Power moved in front of him,
blocking his vanity.
Glory reached for his sword.
Power widened his stance.
Glory made no attempt.
Glory smiled, as he often did,
and in elegant grandeur, he spoke,
"I feel that we're growing,
not visibly, but within.
I noticed at that showing,
They are released from their sin.
They watch for us. Cheer for us.
They wait to begin again.
Wanting it to happen…
They give to us their Passion,
a gift of raw reaction.

A cause is born within them.
They build us in their guts.
For Power and for Glory.
We erupt from within their hearts.
For Power and for Glory.
They are the soul of our story."

"Power and Glory"
Series V
Part II

Power stared at Glory with unreadable eyes.
Then Power swiftly moved.
He laid his hand upon Glory's face.
Power's voice moved through the room.
It was deep and it was stern.
"We are strong together.
We will be stronger yet."
Power turned from Glory,
and stared through the cherry shutters,
down through the window,
down into the crowd.
Hidden in the darkness.
He watched as the crowd diminished.
Power slowly began to speak,
as he watched the masses move.
He pulled his eyes from the window.
His eyes began to shake.
He laid forth the plan.
The story. The epic poem.
For Power.
For Glory.

He had waited so long.
So patient is Power's will.
For all the failure, the slow dismal learning,
Came a time. The rise.
Like a phoenix into the sun.
Power wound his speech down.
His voice hummed through the echoing room.
"Glory shall be spoken upon the streets in every land.

Power shall flow from the lungs of new babes.
We shall give ourselves to them.
They will walk on us like sand.
For Pride and for Faith.
The kingdom is at hand."
Glory smiled as he nodded.
He pounded on the table.
He laughed as he dreamed.
Power laughed back, at twice the tone.
Joy filled the echoing halls.
Power and Glory will rule.

"Power and Glory"
Series V
Part III

Years would pass…
like a flash that was never seen.
Glory's heart grew tired.
Though the masses still gathered.
Though they cheered for Power and Glory.
There was no Power in their passion.
No Glory in their lungs.
They cheered by reflex.
They were common and old.

In a battle, without a name,
Glory stopped and looked up.
He stared at his hand.
It was scarred. It was trembling.
Glory fell without passion.
He fought to the end.
He fell without Hope.
Wheezing in phlegm.

Power held on for awhile.
He was strong 'till the end.
But he went mad. Deeply mad.
He babbled of his Glory.
He babbled for his friend.
No one listened.
Power could not live without Glory.
The people dwindled into sorrow.

Power and Glory faded away.
Power and Glory should have lived.
All should have deeply cheered.
But too rare are those of Power and Glory.
Too rare.   Too forgotten.
But once…once…too long ago to remember…
once…
upon all lips…secure in all hearts…
was the pride of a story…
Deep in the soul--was
Power and Glory.

Chapter 38

Within a Sea of Self

The ranch had grown too loud to think clearly. The girl did not want to sit and overcome the noise. She laughed at herself for choosing the comfort, but still she sat adrift in the Sea of Cortez. Floating. In a calm cluster of blue. The nice thing about the ponga in the Sea of Cortez is that it was too large of a boat to really ever flip over, unless there was a huge storm, but the storms always come in seasons. So she sat and thought in Silence. The slight sound of gentle lapping against the side of the blue and white painted ponga.

The girl loved to stare off in a place where no one wondered why she was staring off. She loved the deep thought process that she had developed. Even if it wasn't real, it was still fun. And very challenging.

As she sunk deeper into herself, she felt an emotional pain. What was the pain? It was only there. Only in the form of pain. There was no definition to what it was. Search. Go deeper. Feel the pain. Maybe the pain will lead to something. Fear comes upon her. But only fear. The pain of fear. So deeper she will go. Sitting through the pain that is telling her that there is something to deal with. Yes. It has been there for a long time. She has felt the disturbance. It is the boy, the one she knew, the one she loved. The one she gave so much to. The epic sensation that she had for him. She knew that she created the sensation. That it had nothing to do with him. It had to do with the freedom she let herself feel. Un-dependent on anything else. She let herself be naked when she wanted to. She let herself be crass and dirty when she wanted to. Even at the ranch she must remain clothed, un-free. It saddens her. She seems free, but those around her are not free enough from their own biases to let her be free. To communicate with them she must hold herself in chains. Do they realize the sacrifice.

Wait.   Go deeper. Do not let the mind distract. The pain.

Aaaaahhhhhhh. That is it. Aaaaahhhhhhh. She gave everything to him. She bared herself, most perfect. She was pure and she existed so. Simply happy, simply at ease. He was not pure. He was an innocent bystander of her pureness. She offered the deepest love, but he was not pure enough to receive it. He was cluttered deeply by the ego. And in the offering of her beauty came the recoiling of his fear of many things, unimportant to her now. *She recorded the event of such greatness with such succinctness. She reached such impressive depths in herself and uncovered an amazing current of love that could flow from her with endless strength. But still his rejection crushed it.* The girl gave him too much. Not too much love, but too much manifestation that he was a part of it.

And so the dam has broken. And emotion poured from her in its rawest form. She could not tell the creature that she truly wanted to let know, how to be free. She could not free him, that which she wanted to love. That she accepted. But the great moment came in a flash, as all do. She realized that he, that ignorant man, broke her heart. He shattered an ego of ideals. He destroyed her. And she never fully realized that. She had noticed her actions were hindered in letting people in to her-self, but now she knows the full reason why. This great young woman that so many are now gathering around performed an act of great cowardice with a simple programmed reflex for her own survival. Her ego exploded to protect her from the pain he had given her. It made her mind forget so much. It couldn't recall the exact sensation of this love. This love she had for all humankind. So purely in those months. It was so fun to love so great. Even when it was horrible to be with him, and horrible to know the people he knew, and horrible to see so much disease. It was the relationship that made it seem great. She used the relationship to enhance her illusion, to hold on to the sensation. And no one has felt close to her because she has not felt free to love them as she felt the freedom of situation to love that foolish boy. She must claim her freedom. She must have it despite anyone.

Love absorbed her. She does not have to be afraid of how others might hurt her.

She must open herself to the pain. She must love the world again. Her control of the world, her need to not be seen so deeply and then rejected again, must end. It must stop and she must, she must, be free. She can accept nothing else. Her heart breaks open again, and it bleeds for all the world. Drink from her blood. Know what she knows. Know love. Know war. Know pain. And know bliss. Know life. Again and again, in ever swelling majesty. Glory flowed through her like the sun across a frozen valley. She roared.
The boat gently rocked in the empty sea.
She laughed. She laughed.
The girl stripped naked. The gentle breeze cooled her flesh. It felt wonderful. She stood in full site. Fully exposed to anyone that might judge her nudity, fully aware of its illegality. She spread open her butt cheeks so the wind could touch her warmest parts. She sighed in free pleasure. She leapt over the side of the boat and sunk into the sea. It felt warm and all encompassing. She could see no land from where she floated, she could see nothing below her or about her, but the tinted green water. She was in a void of uncertainty and surrounding death. And she laughed and she swam.
At ease she would later return to land with a smile that no one dared ask her about. But she wished that they would have asked. The story of facing pain is a good story and to speak it makes it more real. It makes the teller even more vulnerable, because outside opinion is often hard to face. But no one asked. She smiled wider.

"My Majesty"

In the silence of a stone,
In the cause of a war,
In the gaze of the dying,
A world is written,
by the poet of creation.
   A majesty unseen.

In the tears of the gracious,
In the heart of the holy,
is a burning   is a roaring,
of destiny and fate,
of glory and salvation.
A river ever flowing.
Carving forth a life.

It is God in his motion.
Silent.   Never seen.
A definer.   A driver.
A sight for the Blind.

I am the believer.
For the comfort.   For the grace.
I will wait for the carnation
of the love I know so strong.
As is meant for the lonely,
for the man away from flesh.
The flesh of the woman
who saved his darkened heart.
I will burn for her in vigilance.
   A majesty unseen.
I will wait for her carnation.
I will wait to not be damned.

Devoted until the end.
In the Silence when I'm stoned,
In the cause of my War,
In the Gaze of my dying,
She is there.
    A majesty unseen.
She is Here.

Chapter 39

A Simple Will

It had been stored in her mind that in the little town to the north there was a pharmacy. The girl did not know where the information specifically came from but it had a sensation with it that it came from someone else and not herself. At the pharmacy the girl knew that she did not need to have a prescription to buy painkillers. She could pay a small fee for the doctor visit that never happened. It was quite convenient for those that wish to explore the world, or for the others to escape it. ***Blessed be the poor that just need to get by, they often make it freer for all of us because they have less to lose.*** She purchased the prescription and the drugs. Little yellow pills. They looked so tiny, but the girl was assured by a human-like creature they were quite potent. She began with two. She eased them down with a screwdriver at a white-man's bar. Several minutes later she began to feel light and relaxed. It felt nice. Another screwdriver later the girl eased down another little helper. Through the haze she drifted into awake unconsciousness. She talked with people. She had sex with someone. She found a beach somewhere near the water and laid herself down.

From the deep sleep she sensed that she needed to be breathing. The girl had not been pulling oxygen into her lungs. She had been dying. How many pain killers had she taken? The mind had no answers for her as she searched through it. She laid there for a few seconds. She relaxed. The impulse to breath was gone. She had no urge to have to inhale. The reflex was gone. She had to force herself to draw in the air. Her body was shutting down. It was very peaceful. Very easy to die. But she didn't feel like it. She pulled herself out of the tent and walked to the thatch covering of a palapa. She leaned against a pole. She toyed with the sensation of being able to gently walk into death. She didn't force breath for about two and a half minutes. She decided to vomit. The girl focused on the vomit reflex. She tightened her stomach from the bottom up to force everything that was in her belly up to her esophagus. She then pulled the air from her stomach up with her throat. She ejected the death from her body, very systematically. Never feeling any sort of fear. Simply she focused on her decision to live. Each time she wretched, the reflex to breath grew stronger. The acid of her guts burnt into her throat. She overcame the overdose. ***Without fear and with focus the ability to control the body is nearly limitless. Even the choice to leave the body is always open and easily taken. Without fear we can become masters. Or so the girl's axiom echoes through her.***

Chapter 40

A Sick Syndrome

The girl sat in the training plaza and watched a creature she found very beautiful walk throughout a crowd of men that were building small houses. Her looks sculpted well, but still the girl noticed something about the other girl. Even from a distance she could see it in her eyes, in her every unstable movement. There was an excess to it. There was fear in it. But what was the other girl afraid of. There was no threat to her life. Ahhh, yes. Of course.
"Excuse me, sir?."
"Yes me lady," miscellaneous.
"Could you tell that girl over there to please come over here and speak with me."
"Yes, of course." miscellaneous.

She watched as the messenger walked towards the other girl. The other girl was oblivious of the approach. The other girl was too lost to herself. As she was accosted, the girl noticed how the other pulled back slightly, although she was trying to force herself into a superior posture. She was absorbed by her image, of what she should be, of what she desired herself to be.
The other approached the girl and smiled.
"I am glad I finally get to talk to you," a girl.
"Why? What is different about talking to me, as compared to talking to anyone else?"
"You can understand my struggle for freedom," a girl.
"What struggle for freedom?"
"I know you have been watching me. I saw it. You see how they treat me out there. I am trying to help and they won't let me. There is a struggle for equality

right here on this ranch," girl.

"Do you know anything about building houses?"

"No, I never" girl.

"These men have to have these houses built before the storms come."

"Yes, I know. I was trying to help them," girl.

"Do you see all of the scrap and trash in their way? Why don't you move that? Did they ask you to?"

"Yes. But I can help them hold up the walls or nail something in. They just have to tell me how," girl.

"You could have helped them if you only humbled yourself and did the job that was necessary. But instead you inflicted your small tit syndrome..."

"My what?!" the diseased.

Louder, "Your small tit syndrome. Your insecurity. Your disease! Your darkness that spreads across the true freedom like locusts. You are not better than those men..."

"I don't want to be better than them," Diseased.

"You aren't even as good as them! They fight everyday to conquer themselves, so that they are not indirect oppressors like you are. They don't think that they are anything, you think you are something. I saw you trying to fight that man that asked you to come over here in your sick mind. I saw your posture change. I saw you try to control yourself so that he would think that you were strong. You weak fucking bitch! You small titted cunt. How dare you bring your illusions here! And how dare you try to spread your disease. You have found no acceptance here. You have found nothing here. You will take with you pain and rejection and anger and the opinion that I am an idiot, but you <u>should</u> take truth. You should fight through yourself and find the fear that makes you act like this mutation of beauty you are. But you won't. Do not try to speak in response to what I have said. Simply leave. If you do not. I will end your Disease here so that it is stopped from spreading to your spawn or your "friends." Any of these people will think nothing of it to help me dump your body in the sea. You know nothing of equality or even where it truly stems from."

The other girl stood and turned in anger. The girl smacked the other girl's ass. The other turned in insecure rage and stunned silence. "Fuck off bitch."

She offered one last motion so that the other girl would become so

infuriated she would have to face herself. To anyone watching it would have been cruel, but the girl only tried to save the other girl. She only loved what she hated. She loved what the other girl truly was. The real Beauty. But not the Disease that engulfed her. The girl lives in a world that would never accept her, that would never understand a single thing she did. She thought of it for a fleeting second.

She sighed. The girl continued her thought on the conversation.

The lie of equality says that man is equal in beauty, in perfection, in pure whitely clad un-racist perfection. Or so the Dark Society would have you believe. The truth is that man is only equal in the fact that they are all diseased or have been at some point. They are equal in the fact that they exist in the same terms at the root of what they are, beyond the illusions that bind them in this world of disease. They are the same in spirit, in that all men are created equal, as the good man once said. And so, there is no reason to actually hate. We all have been clad in the Disease of Fear, and so are all on the same journey to overcome the lie. It is what all really want, weather they know it in their conscious mind or not. We must think of a single word, "equality," differently. And we must change our entire perception.
She later told this to a soldier that said he hated "them."

Chapter 41

Evolution

Through endless days of thought she unfolded the words for the world. She used the mind to form words, but she did not think from the mind. If she did, she would be trapped by the ego. She used something deeper to trigger thoughts in the mind. She thought from something that she would not dare try to name, for to name it she would have to give it, which would instantly lessen its meaning. And what it was was greater than that. To name it, to classify it, would make it separate from things. But it is not. It is everything. She thought on the lies that warp it.

Evolution. A lie. A speculation that was supposed to separate man from God. The religious hated the theory when it first came out. Fools. They hated it because it threatened their specific power. But it still came from a common place. The new idea still came from the realm that made the concept of God anyway. It replaced God for some, but only in the sense of name and definition. Some used the word "evolution" others used the word "God." Both meant the same thing. It was an alternative for those that could not buy the notion of an unseen God. It served the same purpose. It still made man above all else. It still glorified man as the supreme. It still perpetuated the flow and justification for man to destroy everything that would not bend to his will, to torture the Earth until it yielded up its secrets. Different words, but the same concept. Still arrogant and blind. Both used as justifications for slavery and genocide, for the torturing of nature, for industrialization, for warping the design to keep fear disguised. The disease is everywhere, riddled through so many different thought patterns and ways of life. Enemies of enemies of enemies have it. They all think that they are so different in their vast ranging opinions, but they are all exactly the same. Convince enemies of that. *Do you see the task ahead? Do you see the pain of thought she has. The madness trickles into her, as she walks amongst the haze that forms while trying to explain what is unexplainable. To understand what cannot be explained, one can only become it. It is the curse of enlightenment. There are only so many layers of fear that can be penetrated by truth. If the teacher can convince the fool that the fear that they feel is the disease, or their enemy, or what is "bad," then they can be helped, but often the fear is too strong for the truth.*

Chapter 42

The Calling of Free Men

A group of people sat around her. They were ready for a war. They were ready to serve her. **She could not understand why.** "I see that many of you are ready for war. You want freedom. But you must know that this war will not bring you freedom. We merely take a side. We merely take an opposing side to someone else's side. This war means nothing. It is only a thing to live and die for. It is an accessory to the real war, within our violent selves."

"Then how do we find the rage to fight in this war if it means nothing?" Zarat.

"You teach yourself the technique of raising rage within yourself. Rage is not something that you should have or something that you should be. Understand that it must not own you, but it can be used. I once heard it called 'releasing the animal'. The Apache used to call it that, I think."

"What is the technique?" Zarat.

"I am no teacher of anyone but myself, but I will try to tell you a technique for it. First you must have faced many fears within yourself. You must have the ability to silence your mind so the rage does not rule you, so you do not think that it is what you are, or else you may identify with the rage and you may lose your mind. You don't want to make it what you are, but you must fill yourself with it, tricky. Once you have reached this point, and you may not know if you have, you may be wrong, but so the risks are...anyway, focus your being, your, um, let's see, your consciousness to every part of your body. Perhaps you have been cut on a part of your body and for a second you were fully focused on that part of your body to address the danger to your flesh. In the instant of the cut all else that you think you are was not focused on. Well, if you have felt that then perhaps you can expand that to the full of your body and slightly beyond that if you can.

Then begin to breath very steadily. Forcefully, but slow and steady. Sometimes restricting your throat a bit, with the muscles in your throat helps. You often feel heat inside your chest or your belly. I do not know what names people have for these things."

"Maybe chakras?" person.

"Maybe. But really I don't know if people mean the same thing as I mean by my words or lack of words. But you will notice a clear rise in strength, and you can pull the rage you need from within yourself. You can pull it into your own mind, into your own thought. And this type of rage that I am trying to teach you is controlled and so it has the capability of becoming much stronger than plain emotional rage. You will feel less pain in this state too. Things will actually harm you less. How or why this is, I do not know, but one can see it to a lesser degree in sports after a pep talk. I am not a namer of things. I am not a teacher. I am a destroyer and a creator. I am like the wind. Mindless and destructive, oblivious of my creation"

"Thank you teacher," pupil.

"Thank you teacher. You have taught me much by asking me to explain it to you. I am stronger in this world because you have taught me something. The nameless me."

"Zarat."

"Yes, girl," Zarat.

"Why did you just call me that?"

"You have nothing in this world. Including a name," Zarat.

"You grow in wisdom friend. You are less yourself everyday, and I am pleased to see that."

They laughed.

"I must ask you to do something for freedom."

"As I must," Zarat.

"Zarat, I must ask you to sacrifice yourself to freedom. I must ask you to give everything to it. To let your freedom go and give it to all others. Many people will be free or freer in a physical sense when this is done. But that is because those people that will be free are the masses that are willingly enslaved now. They are the non-thinkers, the slaves that will always be slaves. You know what I mean. I must ask this of you, the only one that I see true sweeping movements of

advancement in, I must ask that you watch over this new world. It is a thankless and pointless job. It is pointless because over time the disease will likely return. And it is those that you free will rebuild oppression again when you are finished. The Disease of Fear, of lies, of fear from death, of existence, and of life. I don't know if we can actually conquer this fear. In fact, we can't. There will be shadows left from the Dark Society. It will be sad when it returns, and it will return unnoticed, undefended, like before. Will you do this? Will you continue what will fail? Will you offer yourself in example to physical slavery?"
"My love, I already have," Zarat.
"Then I will go when I must. Knowing that you will have nothing in this life."
"Thank you, Beloved," Zarat.

178

Chapter 43

For Daddy

Explosive tests were conducted at the far end of the beach. They seemed beautiful from a distance. There destruction too seemed beautiful. Fun. She thought of the times that she would walk with the ranch dog and they would destroy everything as they hiked, from rotting stumps, to carcasses of the dead creatures they would find, to a boulder that exploded as it rolled down a cliff. Not out of advancement or fear, but for fun. It was fun to destroy. The girl enjoys the creatures of nature. ***They understand her.***

...Her thoughts interrupted...She hardly noticed when others were around her.

"The explosives are nearly perfected here. We will make the arsenal in the diseased territory where they must maintain an image of non-oppression. That way we don't deal with the imagined borders. Not that it is hard to get anything across. We could use our drug smuggling contacts, we could easily store what we need in the engines of vehicles, but why deal with it. Besides there is no truck that we can get in Mexico that could be legal in the safety paranoid North, that only cares about money derived from such safety penalties. I hate cops. I hate lies," Dad.
"I suppose there is much to hate."
"Too much," Dad.
"One day, you will find the path to shatter this path. You will find a way to be free from yourself."
"I hope so, but for now I must be this. I must finish the organizing of this physical

war," Dad.

"I think that when it happens, when the decision comes, you will have no choice. You will have to leave it. All of it. And you will understand yourself in time. You will know what everything is. You will see what this war has been. And you will see in yourself the distraction you let happen. And then, the real war will be over. You will be victorious and no one will ever know it."

Chapter 44

The Mountain Home

Many people left the ranch. All but a few to tend the common duties of everyday survival, like the crops and the water systems. They journeyed for a few days, and not in caravan, so they would not draw suspicion. Over a week everyone arrived in the high mountains that the Dark Society claimed to be able to possess.

She had thought little on the explosives that were being built. The destruction itself meant little to her. It is the weak hope that maybe freedom will flow from the war, that maybe their cause would get out beyond it. The girl knows deep down that nothing will come. But in her there must be great hope and great love for the outcome of the war for so much hatred of the disease. She must use the tools created for this world. She must use hatred. She traps herself for the sake of anyone that may someday understand what she is saying. She rages against the disease for the cure. She will use whatever she can. She is waiting for the one to tell the story of the philosophy that she suffered for. The philosophy is her war. She fights to get it out of herself.

In the distance she heard gunfire. She heard the tests and the training of the assault rifles. She thought of how foolish this society was. How arrogant. The common mass of people actually believe that their government is all powerful and knows everything that is happening in the world. Their government can always protect them from people like these that surround her. When in actuality this government is full of all that could not actually make it in the real world of their capitalistic system. It is run by those who were too incompetent and too

cowardly to become blatant criminals and find the wealth and power they always wanted. They have to hide behind titles and armies. Foolish society. Their fear is so strong that they will make themselves believe anything to maintain comfort. "Where there is power, there is evil."
Not noticing those around her. She flinched as he spoke.
"I thought you didn't believe in evil?" boy.
"I don't, ultimately. At the end of things, nothing that happens here, ultimately matters. But "evil" is a word that one can define an enemy with. It is only a word. It just happened to be used. The sentence itself wasn't even directed to anyone, you just happened to hear it. The meaning of the word is different than what it means to others. It means only "bad" for us, in our random fortunes or misfortunes in life. It is not the all encompassing evil of hell or some other illusion of greatness. Power will always breed those that will feed off of the lives of others. Power will breed lies that justify the power to control the masses. It is why there are safety laws and massive police forces here. If there is no populous. If the populous kill themselves, if they don't think that death is horrible, those that have the power will have no one to control. Their power will fall from them. Without people there is no power to have. Doubt anyone that would ever assume authority over you, in any way. They have the mentality to take all freedom from you, that includes your life."
"Isn't it important to not sound contradictory when you speak, when you are trying to teach?" boy.
"If you look for contradiction in wisdom's words, you will find it. When you see into and beyond contradiction, you will find freedom. For example, what is the sound of one hand clapping? And I don't mean the quick closing of that one hand onto itself. That is an idiot's answer."
"............" devoid.
"When you no longer need an answer for the question, when you no longer place your weak human logic to a test to answer the questions of the universe, then you will begin to understand that the questions are the answers. When there is only one answer, you will understand. You will know true intentions, and you will not have the need to attempt to assault someone with your foolish, un-thought logic. There will be no contradiction in your silence. That is where I speak from, and that is what you must understand."

Chapter 45

The Words Grow Fewer as They Are No Longer Needed

"The targets of the assault are common in our minds. But they will be reminded to you now. No organization will penalize the people for their own financial advantage. No 'tickets' or fines shall be extracted from the innocent for the promotion of power. The policing for power will halt. The police units will be purified. Those organizations that have fed on the fortunes of others to promote power and tyranny will fall, taxes must return to a voluntary basis, and hopefully dissolve into its proper unneeded, independent status in the mind's of the Diseased. People must have the right to choose what they want to do with their money; if not, this becomes a land of slaves doing the bidding of the masters. It must also be trusted that there will always be those that will offer themselves for the ease of suffering in the world, people must not be forced to be anyone's perception of enlightenment, including our own. Remember through this war that there is always beauty in in this world, and it is there, in your-self, in your sacrificed hearts.

All organizations that manage land and penalize those that dare use it, will be destroyed. To deny any person a space to exist in is to imprison them to a system they may not wish to belong to. (And remember not belonging to the system is different than not wanting to live in a certain place in any imagined country.) To make someone a working slave so that they can simply and barely afford the rent on a place to exist is tyranny. Remember the rights of man, "Life, Liberty, and Property." There is a strong reason that Locke included property in his statement. All organizations that kill indiscriminately and cease the built lives of free people to place power and possessions in their own hands must be stopped. There are organizations in this Dark Society that are designated the false right to cease a person's right to defense and the right to be dependent only on themselves, these organizations are so corrupted with the lust to sustain their place in this society that they can auction off the properties they have ceased to sustain their own power. All with complete immunity to their actions. Man has been placed above man and we are slaves for it. Once the tax organization even ran a brothel that they once condemned to gain more and more power. They must oppress to succeed. As do the organizations that deny the right to warp perception through the use of hallucinogenics. Their reason being that it would warp our sense of reality so much that we would see beyond the lies that their way is the only way to see.

We are also granted the right through our very existence to pursue happiness by whatever means necessary. It is our will that makes all of these things possible, not a decree. Our will to be free is what must make us free. Remember that it is your choice and no one else's. These organizations remain nameless to us because they are the same branches of tyranny that have appeared in all societies that the Disease takes. They merely have different names. We will not enforce the illusions the Dark Society has built around these names through endless years of propaganda and publicity. We will stop what has become. We will end what should have never been. If it seems like our numbers are few, if you feel like we may not succeed, then remember that you have nothing to lose, you already don't have freedom. So you do not have yourself. You are not your own master. And remember that the majority of all revolutions, including the one that first founded this Dark Society from light was led by less than one percent of the population. So have faith and fight strong. Fight for yourself and all that you will never imprison. Destroy. And cease no power. For Freedom, end all that assume authority over anything," Zarat.
The true heroes appear from a force unrecognized and barely identifiable. These servants create techniques in those that have the will to fight. They offer the techniques of hope and faith for those too weak or ignorant to know how to create it themselves.

Peace overcame the girl as she knew that her cause had been passed to another. To another seer, one of great talent and a fine user of the world. Her work was nearing its end. Soon she will be free, again.

Chapter 46

Loving

The girl stared somewhere to the left of oblivion, just slightly into Hell. There was something that diverted her attention from purity. A struggle she had felt all her life. One that had been eased at times, but returned again and again. Death. Killing. She, herself, had killed. She had inflicted fear. She had done the very thing she tries to stop. She gave pain...Wait...She gave nothing. Those that chose to fear death felt fear. It is this that she is trying to stop. The fear that we choose. To tell everyone that it is a choice to fear. It is their own weakness that enslaved them. They chose poorly. *A layer of anger fell away, as she rationalized the point of anger away*. Anger. Anger. There is anger for what she had to be in a life. A bringer of destruction. When all she wanted was to bring love. Peace. Why did something have to be destroyed? Death. Death. Death. Death. Death. Wait. That's right. She had died before. She had felt what is important. The girl felt it in the water. She had felt the great joke. She had felt that nothing these foolish silly lying humans take seriously is important. No matter what you "gain" in life, you still return to what is important. You still have the pure loving, unhindered by the ego...the self. You still are that self that is forever. Un-owned. Unnamable. Deeper than the mind. Grander than fleeting power. Death. Death. Death. Death. It comes to us all. People ruin their lives and the lives of so many others because they fear it, because they do not understand it. Silly. Silly death. It is not important. People observantly base every decision they have on the fear of a tiny thing. Of tiny death. On a huge lie that death is bad, and should be avoided. The lie says that what is held in life is what we are and we lose that, our things, our friends, our family. We are nothing. Silly. Comically silly. We are everything and that never changes. We are nothing? How absurd. How bloody silly. She laughed. She laughed again. Loudly, she laughed. She stared down into oblivion. Sweet tender all encompassing oblivion. Unafraid to not "exist," as she has been told is so important. Too many are afraid to look into oblivion, the possibility of not existing, that their lives are ruined in a mad scramble to have to be secure. To have to hang on. If there is no fear of death, there is no fear of not having. There is no fear of anything. Humans would not need anything. No one could give them anything. If humans did not need anything, if they did not have to have, anything, no one would be able to gain power over them. There would be no power. There would be no tyranny. The Dark Society would not be able to rise again. There would be freedom without fear. To hang on to the Dark Society is the manifestation of deep fear. The deep fear of not having, when in fact we need nothing. If people could only know.

People spend their lives worrying about it foolishly. They hear for their whole lives that death is something to be feared. It is something to be avoided at all costs, and "you" must do everything to prolong the lives of everyone around you. Suicide is bad. Dying is bad. We are programmed with the fear from everyone who selfishly "loves" us. It is not that big of a deal. You only lose everything on Earth, you don't lose anything important. You lose greed. You lose the ego. You lose the silly fear of death that yields all other fear and limits to a life. It is why we don't take risks. It is why we don't enjoy. You lose material. Bad people, cowards, tell lies about death and they spread it through all society. These people do this, because there is no power for them if there is no value on life. Fear mongers need people to have power. Butter knives are curved so that people would quit stabbing each other at dinner, because the "King" was losing to many valuable disciples. They need lives to feed from. If there are no people, there is no power. We are taught to fear death by those that want power, by those so afraid that they need power. Freedom is now. It is always now. It is our choice to take it

Love. Freedom. Eternity. She knows what it is. She had always known, but she too can be distracted by the plays of the ego. Nothingness is what she is. Nothing to fear. Nothing to lose. Nothing to gain. She is already complete. She always had been. No decision is to be feared. No life is shameful. Not in the end. It all comes from the same source. The source it never really left. It is warped through fear. But all paths are towards freedom. To love. All things are ultimately free. And whatever comes before or after death means nothing. It shall be dealt with from the same source. Without fear no Heaven or Hell could ever reign us, just as no savior or tyrant of Earth could. Freedom. Freedom. Love. nothing.

She sat away from the camp. Feeling the vibration of the music. The crowd celebrated, perhaps for a last time, perhaps not. "Hello," came a gentle voice that broke the girl away from the sinking sensation of stretching eternity. The girl wiped the drool from her mouth and turned to see a finely curved figure in the darkness of the night.
"Hello."
"I just wanted to see if you were as beautiful as everyone said you were," gentle woman.
"Am I?"
"Epically," kind woman.
"You hold a beauty about you as well. A sensation. May I touch your skin?" ***The girl asked not for lust, but to feel the beauty. To revel in its greatness.***
"If I may touch yours," beauty.
The beauty sat down across from her. The girls' hands reached towards the face of the other. "Your skin is like suede. So soft," beauty.
"Yours is like a human's. May I smell your neck?"
"If I can smell yours," Beauty.
Gently they leaned in towards each other, with the innocent awe of an explorer walking into Eden. Their cheeks brushed as they easefully pulled in one another's sweet scent. The girl kissed the Beauty's neck, like a log floating on the top of the sea with no guided course of its own. The kisses were returned for the sake of the sensation of loving. It seemed to cover them in the chilly night. Gently the clothing of the other slowly slid into the dirt. The girl had never seen breasts so enticing, so full and soft. She rubbed her cheek against them. She smelt deeply her lover. She sunk slowly down into the hair that surrounded the Beauty's sensation. She breathed deeply in the scent of dripping pussy. The

musk was so thick in its scent that she tasted it in her mouth. She took casual notice of her own fluids running down her leg. She pressed her face through the Beauty's pubic hair until her mouth could open and let her tongue sink invitingly into the lover's gentle moist bloom. The girl ran her hands down the back of the Beauty and down the curve of her wonderful ass. The girl's hand's fingers reached into the Beauty's ass-crack and seeped a finger into her asshole as her tongue shoved fully into her tasty pussy. ***How blessed that in this time, so close to the release, she was able to move enough away from her anger towards the society, that she thought she had to hang onto, so that she could make such love. The only place she was on the flesh of that nameless Beauty that pleased her soul with unbiased grace.***

They lay in the night for endless hours. With nothing but time to play with each other's bodies. Playful happy sex. Without the nausea of control or inhibition. They rolled forth with fantasy and chat. Casually licking or fingering whatever they wished. Kissing each other with fingers sunk deep inside each other. In the bliss of touch they danced through un-owned love. Love merely existed in that space of indefinable time. A memory to be remembered, without thought, in sensation only.

Chapter 47

Technique

Soon the time will come upon the assembled groups that chose to fight. A chill ran through her body. It ran through her not because of the thought but because her naked body was swept over by a wind. One can set the mind to have to feel nothing, to make the body feel no pain. She had performed exercises before. She sat in a fight against and for her own abilities to create all her own reality. She focused on the center of her chest, while letting all thoughts primarily fall away. ***She knew that to meditate for enlightenment is different than to meditate for technique. For technique the mind can be slightly present, it is the focusing of energy that is important for physical technique.*** The girl's breathing slowed, but it maintained force and focus. Her mind encompassed the color of fire. Orange and red. She felt warmth from her center, from the place that the physical heart inhabits.

She let the thought of cold being harmful to her fall away. She chose to not believe that it could kill her. By this point she could not allow it to even enter her mind, although it recently had, moments before meditation began. But this is a different time entirely. She is a different person in every second. Just as we all are, but she notices it. As the heat grew stronger within her she noticed that her feet and hands still held a strong chill. It was harder to focus heat to these areas. Is the soul centralized? Is there a stronger point of energy? She tried to imagine yellow heat channeling through her body with the rhythm of her breath. It eased the cold in her extremities after several minutes. The girl will need more practice at this. The technique is not strong yet. But she will let herself now go into the other type of meditation. She will look into herself and attempt to retain the heating technique. Silence... She feels she is still imperfect. Not quite what she could be. She could be better. Fear rises again and again. Where does it come from? She finds fear for the war. Not for death. For the success of it. She feels the folly that could occur. All the "goodness" it is based on must use the techniques of the Dark Society to succeed. What may be asked of her if there is a v ctory? How could she rule when she is only a servant? Fear swept her like the cold breeze and the heat in her dwindled for a second. She refocused and went deeper into herself. This is fear. A fear to succeed. Why did it rise again? Another fear. Dammit. What must she focus on to have no fear? What? Relax. Go deeper into peace. *She routes her true consciousness with audio hallucinations, with words, with emotions, with visions, with energy. Everything that "human" is can be used for our own mastery.*

In the knowledge of non-attachment, found only in the silence, she remembered what she first had to, when first she was fighting herself. "It does not matter what happens. I can gain nothing and I can lose nothing." *She used "I." She identified herself as "I" because she referred directly to her being, her essence, the thing called soul. Not the girl, but what allows the girl to be. In the journey of uncovering the self through the haze of the disease one must repeat the same mantras again and again every time a new part of the disease is revealed. It is the dedication of a saint.* "In the end I can own nothing. I can have nothing. There is only death and freedom from what can be owned. The constant is all that matters in the universe and the eternity. It is the final number, what all equations are a part of." So what is there? What is here? What can the girl know? The girl can know that there is only now, as there has always been regardless of what she may think tomorrow could be or what yesterday might have been. There is no fear of what may come or what has come. The being, the existence, is always only now. It never gains, it never loses, it never changes. It is always. It is the center of the universe for all being and infinity always extends from it and throughout it. *The searcher of true freedom and the victim of the disease both temper and meld themselves all their lives to be what they think they should be. One must know that he is a liar and one must strive to be honest, to unravel the mystery of the dysfunctional ego. The mind repeats everything again and again with only slight change. The vast difference between the two minds is that one fights to hang on while the other fights to let go. One mind is possible in its goals, the other never will be, even if it found immortality in the human form.* The girl can know that she is nothing and everything. Focus only on the now, what is, without past or future, without lies applied by interpretation. Nothing could ever harm her. Nothing ever has. Beyond the veil of fear she can only find herself. *Conscious mantra; Live now. There is nothing to lose. There is nothing to gain. There is only now.* This is the truth. Since this is the truth, two paths are revealed. One can sit and do nothing so that love is the only thing that can flow from their self or one can dive into living and choose to do everything. The girl rationalizes that we are on earth to be a part of life. Or else we would not be in the physical world at all. So, she chooses to experience the fortune of being in this reality without hindrance, without paying heed to the fearful lies that have always told her she cannot do whatever she wants. This is the path that the man Siddhartha faced and the character Zarathustra faced. The only difference in their being is that one chose to be only with the Way, with the Being, with "God," and the other chose a balance so as not to insult his own existence in the physical world. It is a fleeting time. And everything or anything can be done. We have already won all that we can. So she will live and she will die, without regret and without ever knowing or being concerned with what she will leave behind. Whatever she could leave behind in the physical world would remain irrelevant, eventually and ultimately. The girl is not a god, she is only what "god" is.

Slowly she emerges from the meditation. Her mind brushes a thought. She had no fear of success. She was wrong. She fears her opportunity to take power. To replace the Dark Society with another reflection of it. She will focus on her path. She will choose simply to have no power. She will simply choose to have nothing. She will have no society. She will not create something that must be fed by the bodies of human slavery. She will only be good to all she can. The girl will be a society unto herself.

Chapter 48

Just Another Physical War

The explosives ripped their fiery hand through the town. Lighting the shaded streets with avenging rage. Then came the wait. The wait for the forces. The wait for the armies of police that were sure to come. The sirens reached the ears of the revolutionaries from the distance. The combat vehicles ran down upon its Citizens to defend themselves and secure their place once again. Explosives lodged underneath the streets tore up into the metal. The stench of burnt flesh made most of the hero's/murderer's noses flinch. Parts of men scattered around them. ***They could have destroyed them all with the secondary explosives but that is not what they wanted to do. Some things would have been incomplete.*** Then came the first charge while the police were stunned. It was important for the revolutionaries to touch blood. To kill from a distance would only open the way for the coldness of the disease to creep in, of arrogance and delusions of grandeur. To take life with the hands puts more perspective into the sense of life and openly tells of the importance of not fearing death. Death takes us in confusion and stammering futility. It is the girl's wish that they see lifelessness in a dead body while they feel the warmth of what life was on themselves. The fighters had to feel the circle of their life as they felt the thrill of believing they could make a majestic difference by reclaiming their society. ***An experience.***

While flesh was cut around the girl, she stood still in chaos. Unafraid of chaos. She gave into the rising bliss she knew. She took special notice of the heat rising from the burning buildings and men around her. If everyone was not so afraid and full of adrenaline they too would see the beauty in an event they may never

see again. The glow on the streets. The dance of the shadows. The fling into the fury of survival. So incredibly pointless
thought, but thus was her course. Now she let it sweep over her. The silence. Everything seemed to slow.

She took part in combat. Her movements were graceful as if led by music translated straight from the root of her existence so that she may feel in the thralls of life. Through a wisp of smoke she saw the man she called Father. It was now that she let her game go. She was glad the father played along with her lie to him. She was happy he always knew it was a lie. The man was smart and he was hilarious to the girl. She was glad the egos met, and he was advanced enough for the pretending that expanded them both. A child can call anyone "father," but the child never really knows who they call father, as it is for the ignorant father that speaks "daughter" or "son." The girl never knew her father, but as a child. She hardly knew the man that played her lie that swung his sword in front of her now. ***The father does not know why it was him, but she lays a trap that offers him a gift and a duty.*** He fought frantically, not yet knowing what this battle truly was. He swung without identifying what his sword absorbed. She watched the dance of his ego try to defend itself. She laughed at it. She laughed. The love for all that existed, in every action anything performed. Her fear went to nothing, to not even being a concept. She marveled at the dance. Its simplicity. Its ease of escaping it. The joy of letting life exist. And not taking that life personally, not adding lies to circumstance.
At this moment it occurred to her that this war would solve nothing at all. Of course not, she always knew it would fail, but she never fully understood until the second she existed in absolute, peaceful nothingness, beyond the first lies of bliss. As she dissolved beyond herself, the girl realized that it is true freedom unattached from all of this madness that is a far more worthy thing to have than the freedom from the heavy hand of oppression in this foolish physical world. She knew she could escape it all within herself. She felt no need for violence. She felt no need to bring pain. She wanted only to bring love. But she also did not feel inclined to stop the flurry of death that was so amusingly all around her. It had always been, since time dawned. The same struggle, all of us against each other. And she could not stop it anyway.

She walked in a flurry of her giggles and waves of deepening delight towards the father-man she saw drenched in blood. Such a pretty rarely seen color of red.
"What is she doing?! Zarat! What is she doing?! She is not fighting! Zarat?!" soldier.
"Shut up! She understands things you cannot possibly imagine. Keep fighting! Let her be," Zarat.
As she approached the man with the sword, she took a small knife from her pocket and raised to touch the man. She noticed a flower on the ground. How strange that a flower would be here. She reached her knife outward into the father's shirt and slightly nicked his back. He turned in a rage of survival and landed his sword onto the girl's gentle skull. Like all things, she lived, she fought, she thought, she believed and she died completely in isolation and totally alone. It is not sad. We all journey alone, through ourselves, through our minds, encompassed by our own existence. She just had the strength to realize it and use it for the joy that echoed in her skull as the bliss of death cracked it open and set her free once more, from the madness and the tyrants, to be a full part of everything she truly loved.

She committed a type a suicide, but a suicide that transcended suicide itself. She had no need for death, but she had no need for life. It was not a cowardly response. Before the death was delivered, her mind functioned in a distant place, like an echo she could hear in a valley that laid just outside her vision. The mind laughed at the selfishness that many she had touched would feel. It laughed at the weakness they would not know they were displaying. It laughed at what she left for me. The mind knew that tears were coming for her. But she did not care. Any pain that would have been caused to people left in the swirls of lives like her followers or lovers is their own fault. It is their greed of want. Wanting her. Wanting her to live for their own selfish satisfaction. There are so many made up of greedy fear, trapped in blind cowardice. Her final thought was how the Dark Society must be overcome. It must be overcome by the brave that hear only the full voice of their peaceful hearts through the midst of the endless violence that we are.

Chapter 49

The End

I hold her bloodied head in my hands. The interior of my hands feel so cold. It is such a contrast to the warmth of her blood on the outer part of my flesh. What a pretty red. Split wide. Her skin is so soft, like a fabric never made before, but similar to suede. My thumb almost sticks to it as I feel it. She has a pretty eye. I thought on her life. I thought of the sadness the slaves would feel on her life. I dropped her head on the cobble street. It made a thwapping thud, like a watermelon being dropped from standing height. I noticed as I turned away that it split open more greatly. I walked away. I began to forget about the blood on my hands. Blood grows so cold on the hands, so quickly. I always found it strange the way coldness deepens in the hands from an outside wetness. It seems like heat should come from within, not cold from without. I might remember her. Maybe when I wash my hands again.   She was something different. I saw it in her just before I killed her. I saw everything in her. Like a flash as I held her. Her story seeped into my own. It burned me. It felt good to be touched by something. It is good to know that something that free had existed. I feel good. I feel everything about her. I feel her thoughts, her mind, I feel the essence of her, the very impulse that commands thoughts to be, the sensation of being that exists before and between every thought. I feel that pureness and that awareness that could dare notice such a location of the self. I feel her. I like her. I think I will remember her. I will remember. I will remember her life as she remembered it. I walk onward through the shaded sun of the trees. What a beautiful day it is..

Chapter 50

The Beginning

Within us all is the Dark Society. Within us all is the potential for darkness. First we must admit that and then we can prevent it. If we run from ourselves, if we forgive ourselves or think that we are forgiven through worship, the darkness will spread forth from our very beings and encompass a society and the society will always try to encompass the world and whatever else it can acquire beyond that. See yourself through the eyes of the girl. See yourself in her hatred for you. See that you are not what you dreamt to be and that you have become everything you hate in everyone else. See what you are doing to the people you love, can you even feel it anymore? And so, see yourself in her love of what you can be. If victory within the darkness of ourselves is not reached then the dark society will return endlessly, as it always has, to try to persuade the world to worship it. When people lust for power and security from fear it grows, from generation to generation. From Egypt to Rome, to Greece to the White Church, to Russia, to the Black Superiority, to the United States of America, to anyone wanting power or money or image, and from all other societies that were wiped from certain histories with smears of blood and burning flesh unleashed by a forgotten people that thought they had no other choice. Darkness shall cover the earth like a wind across a field wherever there is a need for power over anything. Only when we realize that the control we think we have shall never give us what we look for in our blind fury of a fleeting life will we know the society without tyranny. Only then will you not be the oppressor. Only when our hearts are eternally vigilant in stillness shall the blindness never return. When it is realized that societies are created and destroyed from the same horrible needs again and again will we see that the destiny of the world is in our own hearts. Given by choice, to control nothing, but be everything. To know freedom, granted to ourselves, and relinquished by nothing but fear.

Definition: Vastness: Everything and nothing, all at once.

For everything you have freed me into, I will write for you the Great Book. The first book about one of our minds. I will tell the story you have told me. I will tell of your madness and your bliss and how you suffered to try and free us all. I will tell about that deepening silent sensation given to me by the beauty that is The Girl.

Calmness

A Class On How To Not Worry

Presented by Instructor Stephan Pacheco

Who grants peace: You do, no one else can give it to you.

What we seek: Emptiness, Stillness, Peace.

When do we seek it: Now, always now, always in the instant, constantly.

Why: Through the pursuit of emptiness we can bypass the illusions of the mind that distract us from truth. Meaning, we gain the ability to turn off the psychological defenses that we use to seek approval, comfort and control.

Note: Any disturbance or discomfort we feel is the root of something negative (like insecurity, fear, anger, hatred, loneliness, etc.) within ourselves, not "bad", but negative to our perfect lives. From a point of silence we can learn to guard our minds and ease the suffering we bring to others and ourselves through the negative use of the wanting ego.

How to: (In a group it is easier to utilize spiritual energy, because it is naturally shared among the participators. Plus, people naturally want to adapt to their surroundings.)
We focus inwards. We remove the focus of consciousness from the forehead and eyeball area. It is good to rest the focus into the stomach, but avoid applying pressure to the physical system; meaning, keep it light, the spiritual consciousness is light energy, it does not require force, it is relaxed. Focus on stillness. If a thought arises, perhaps this is a sign to go deeper. More still. Present. If one feels despair or anxiety, perhaps this is a sign to feel the emotion, do not think of it, feel it and let it dissolve. Let

it lead you deeper as you relax it. We can also direct our minds within this meditation, because we have separated ourselves from the mind and are now more able to control it, so, we can utilize the technique of the Inner Smile. The Inner Smile is a sense of happiness that we can draw across the void of nothingness/stillness that we are seeking. We must focus on our body as an empty shell. More and more empty. More and more into the void. Trusting all along that there is no danger in doing this. You can't stop existing and there is no damnation. Focus more and more that the world around us is an illusion, and we are an empty shell within the illusion. We know that we are doing this correctly because our tension will become less and our sinuses will clear.

What this does for us: Brings us peace, and lets us stop making war with others to prove that we are right and that we are in control. We are able to not fear losing control. And when we are very still we can see that all around us is the same stillness from within ourselves, it is simply masked by the hectic ego that fears its own death.

Note: If you feel yourself becoming sleepy, open your eyes a third of the way and look to the tip of your nose or at a random point in the space in front of you. Do not look at an object. Or, focus more deeply on the empty shell and energy should enter your body. One should not feel sleepy if this is done correctly.

*single page 8.5x11 "fridge" version printable at http://www.libertycore.org

Know the Author

Stephan's ties to his characters are deeply personal, because they are a symbol of his very mind and his direct experiences towards life. Born on the Day of the Entertainer, June 7th, Stephan's path was tied early to the audience's arousal and whims, which likely contributes to his catalystic writing styles. A crowd favorite on stage, he performed in more than 100 productions from the age of eleven, often cast as a figure of power or intensity. Yet at the age of fourteen his creative intellectualism would take on a deciding definition. For as he died in the depths of the water, like (*his*) She did, he felt what it was to not be entangled by the threats of man, to know that he was Free, and all forms of power were lies, just like the identity he witnessed shed floating in the water. And in that, he learned that he could even be free from himself, and he saw the point that people reason from and the husk-like corpse they are violently and frantically defending. This is what he was able to realize about his own Existence. His meditation, his message, his concerns and his passions lead few to challenge his commitment to a world that is Universally Free, and he reasons our minds towards it, his Becoming, his vision of Existentialism. He will expose us to the world, all the parts we don't know how to accept, and he'll effectually show us that the world has no Evil in it, and that Equality is permanent and the mind is constructible because interpretations are malleable. Stephan realized this in his own death. He could aim at any point, and direct his mind in any direction, and see any situation as he chooses to veil it. And the less veils he uses, the less he demands from the world, the more beautiful he says it becomes and the more he is forced to show us what is spilling from his imagining heart, so that we can laugh and play and prosper, without fear of our own independently forced Evolution.

Composed by Samuel Drake

Coming Soon...

The struggle for Freedom continues, as interpreted through the faculties of:

<u>Zarat</u>
Notes of the Becoming
Story by Zarat

Four years later Zarat struggles against the angst of his post war reality. He manifests a war within himself and wills the struggle against the specific reality behind the sneers, the fingers and the disapproval in the eyes of the individuals and groups that inhabit the Dark Society. All the while struggling with the relationship that changed his life. His differing interpretations shedding new light and understanding on the mysterious Girl that changed his soul and bent his life.

and in...

<u>Existentialism</u>
A Solution
Story by The Father
Compiled by The Priest

The Father poetically describes the vast tapestry of his manifested life, revealing his past and his encounters, with women, actors, the Free and the Tyrannical. Inviting his Friends, his listening audience, in once more to see the beauty of his passionate spirit. Although the Father's mind fades to the grip of dementia, he is driven to develop his Final Solution. In the course of his reasoning he will reflect across his massively moving life, from his years of fame, to his encounters with the Girl and Zarat, where far more is revealed about the interaction of the Three, as he unravels the mystery of a familiar Humanity.

See where the Conclusion of this multi-part series truly begins in these coming Titles.